GLIMMER OF DECEPTION

OTHER REALM, BOOK 4

BY HEATHER G.HARRIS

DEDICATION

For my dearest one,
who always supports me.

CHAPTER 1

M Y HELL HOUND barked determinedly at my boots and I groaned. 'Quit it,' I said to Gato, throwing a pillow roughly in his direction.

My head hurt. Too much wine.

He didn't quit it. I pushed myself up and glared at my insolent dog. He ignored my death gaze and kept on barking at my favourite pair of ankle boots. I heaved myself up and flounced over to them. Then I let out a horribly girly scream and leapt back onto the bed. 'What the hell?' I shouted at Gato. 'Why is there a mutant spider in my shoes?'

He gave me a look that could only be termed smug.

'All right, all right, you were right to tell me about the demon spider,' I conceded. I looked around my bedroom for a likely looking spider container. Not a damn thing. 'I'll go to the kitchen and grab some Tupperware. You keep the spider pinned down there.'

Gato gave a woof of acknowledgement and focused all his attention on our eight-legged friend.

I grabbed my phone and took a couple shots of the

big guy. Always documenting; it's a private eye's habit. Evidence secured, I ran downstairs and searched through the kitchen cupboards. I had a tinfoil take-away box with a cardboard lid for if I wanted to batch cook and freeze some dinners. Not that I was much of a chef, but my occasional room-mate Hes was.

I stabbed the cardboard lid a few times to give the little critter some airholes, big enough to breathe through but not big enough to crawl out of, then raced back upstairs. As I ran, I gathered my intention. I burst into the room and focused it on the spider. 'Up!' I ordered.

It leapt out of my black suede boot and into the air. 'In!' I held out the container. The spider flew into it, and I squealed a little as I secured the lid. With shaking hands, I placed the box on my dresser and let out an explosive breath. 'Damn – that was massive.'

Gato ducked his head in agreement.

The spider was nearly the size of the palm of my hand. Its legs were thick and hairy, and it was a muddy-brown colour, save for a splash of red across its terrifyingly large jaws. It had a lot of beady eyes, two of which were bigger than the others. I swear it had glared at me as it flew through the air. And the flying seemed all wrong – since when could spiders fly?

Catching the beast had cleared the hangover right out of my system, so that was a plus side to a horrific experience. I spent the next five minutes Googling spiders and scrolling through images of terrifying arachnids. Spiders just aren't my thing.

I was glad no one but Gato had been around to witness my screams because my street cred would have gone down the toilet. Not that I had much to start with, but I'm pretty sure I got some from my association with Emory, King of Dragons and miscellaneous other creatures.

There was an impatient tug on my bond from Emory. In the heat of the moment, I'd ignored two previous tugs. I wasn't *au fait* with this bond that now connected us, and I wasn't sure how to reply, so I texted him. *I'm ok. Just a spider. x*

I was downplaying the experience. According to Google my visitor was a Brazilian Wandering Spider, considered to be the deadliest spider in the world.

I'm an Occam's Razor girl; I believe the most likely explanation is going to be the correct one. The nearest places the spider could have come from were Chester Zoo or Knowsley Safari Park but a quick online search didn't reveal any headlines about escaped wildlife. I doubted the Wanderer could have found its way onto a plane and all the way from Brazil to Liverpool airport then to my house by itself. The chances were that someone had planted it in my room deliberately; *ipso facto*, someone was trying to kill me.

I brightened. An assassination attempt; just what I

needed to get a shot of perspective.

I'd been moping for the last few weeks ever since Bastion had dropped the bombshell that my parents had hired him to kill them. That had been a serious headfuck, and I'd been submerged in malaise and misery. The only things that made me feel better were drink or Emory. I knew that Emory was worried about me because our bond let me feel his concern. I felt guilty that my mood was affecting him but, selfish prick that I was being, not guilty enough to do something about it.

That ended right now. I had a mystery to solve: someone was trying to kill me with an exotic spider. I grinned. The game was afoot.

As I saw it, I had two options for dealing with the Brazilian Wandering Spider: one was to call pest control, the other was to call someone who would look after it. I didn't want to kill the little bugger just for being in the wrong suede boot at the wrong time, so I dug up some details on the British Arachnological Society.

Their website had a handy index of spiders but my red-jawed mate wasn't there. The clue was in his name – he obviously wasn't British. Even so, the society might be able to help. I uploaded the picture I'd taken of him and hit send. If they didn't get back to me in an hour or two, I'd call the zoo. I didn't want to keep the fella in a tinfoil box for long, air holes or not, because he didn't have much room. I'm an animal lover and that affection apparently extends to scary spiders – when I'm not freaking out.

I gave Gato a pat. 'Good work on the spider detecting. I think he's a Brazilian Wandering Spider, the deadliest spider in the world.' I grinned. 'I've pissed someone off enough that they want to kill me. Isn't that great?'

Gato's look was full of scorn.

'What?' I asked. 'It's been boring around here since Bastion told me my parents hired the hit on themselves.'

Gato hunched over and let out a low whine.

'I'm okay,' I said firmly. 'I'm over it.' *Lie.* My radar pinged loudly and I sighed; just once, I wanted to be able to lie to myself. 'Alright, maybe not over it completely but I'm done with this depressive shit. I am officially moving on.'

Gato's eyes were disbelieving.

I took a deep breath and raised something that had been pulling at the edges of my mind for the last few weeks. 'We could go to the Third realm,' I suggested. 'A little hop back into the past, and we could ask my parents why they did it.'

Gato whined and shook his head. I felt deflated. 'Yeah,' I said with false cheer, 'I guess you're right. I don't want to get lost in the Third realm like Leo Harfen. That is one muddled-up elf. Besides, what if I went back to the wrong time and found out that I'd said the wrong thing and sent Mum and Dad down the whole death path to begin with?' I grimaced.

Gato looked at me with puppy-dog eyes.

I forced a smile. 'It's fine,' I said firmly. 'No bother.'

Gato is my hell hound and my portal to the other realms. If he didn't want me prodding around in the Third realm, I wasn't going to argue. Some leader of the pack I was.

My phone rang and interrupted my musings. An unknown number flashed up. I answered it professionally, just in case. 'Sharp Security, Jinx speaking.'

'Hi … er, Jinx. Is this the lady with Brazilian Wandering Spider?'

'That's me,' I affirmed cheerfully.

'I'm Sebastian, from the British Arachnological Society?' He said it like a question. He should really have known who he was.

'Hello, Sebastian. What should I do about this spider?'

'Is it contained?'

I slid my eyes to the silver prison on my dresser. 'Yup.'

'Great.' He gave a relieved sigh. 'I checked the photo you sent, and it's definitely a Brazilian Wandering Spider. Are you happy for me to assist in its relocation?'

'I'd be downright delighted.'

'Good. I've already contacted a colleague in Chester Zoo. Can you give me your address?'

I reeled it off. 'Someone will be with you within the hour.' Sebastian cleared his throat. 'It's considered quite a dangerous spider. Don't let it out.'

I bit back the urge to make a smart-alec comment. The guy was helping me for free. 'I won't. Thank you for your help, I really appreciate it.'

'A Brazilian Wandering Spider,' he repeated wonderingly then rang off without a goodbye. Spider nerds had lousy phone manners, or at least this one did.

'Help is coming,' I said to Gato. 'Let's grab some breakfast.'

I was suddenly ravenously hungry; there was nothing like an adrenaline rush to kick start the body. I checked the time and grimaced: 9 a.m. The day had started without me. I hadn't been looking after myself, and I'd been a lousy half-mate to Emory. Poor guy. Well, they do say in sickness and in health… I'd make it up to him.

My stomach demanded a bacon sandwich, which was well within the limits of my culinary skills. I chucked extra bacon into the grill for Gato – we both deserved a big breakfast. I checked my work emails while I ate, firing off a few responses to clients and a request for background check for Hes to run when she had a chance.

A knock on the door interrupted my work reverie. Spider guy, I hoped. I opened the front door. Spider guy was a spider gal with green hair, a nose piercing and a friendly smile. She was carrying a clear plastic terrarium.

'Hi, I'm Clarissa. I'm here about a spider?'

'Great, I have one of those.' I let her in and left her in the lounge while I fetched my hairy companion from my bedroom. She grimaced a little at the tiny box. 'Sorry, it was all I had that I could make air holes in,' I apologised.

She slid back the lid of the plastic terrarium and laid the silver box inside it. Using a pen, she hooked it into one of the air holes and whisked off the lid before sliding home the clear top of the terrarium. She clicked it locked on both sides and then looked into it. 'It really *is* a Brazilian Wandering Spider.'

'Yup,' I agreed. 'You'll take good care of it?'

'Of course. We just need to fill out some paperwork to show you've donated it to the zoo.'

The forms didn't take long and soon Clarissa was making her way back to her VW Beetle with a spring in her step. I'd made her day, which made me feel pretty good. I didn't have a deadly spider in my house any more, which made me feel even better.

Today was looking up.

CHAPTER 2

AFTER SPIDERGATE I was feeling pretty upbeat. Sure, someone might be trying to kill me but I'd rescued an exotic spider and packed it off for an exciting life in a zoo. Riding my high, I decided to go for a run. Running always brings me some perspective and a positive buzz; exercise is my friend, and I'd been neglecting it these last few weeks.

The crisp February air was cool but the sun was peeking its way through some wispy cloud, warming my skin and helping to lift my mood. I was in danger of feeling happy. It had been weeks since my last run and I winced at the obvious decrease in my fitness levels. A few weeks off was all it took to see a massive reduction in my pace, and my muscles were protesting. I listened to them reluctantly. I'd injured myself running before, and the recovery time was always such a pain in the ass – or, in that case, the groin.

Still, I was five kilometres in and my time wasn't bad. Twenty-seven minutes was nothing to sniff at for most people. I felt reassured that I was still in good shape, albeit not my best shape. A few more weeks and I'd be fighting fit again.

I asked Gato to portal me back to the Common realm. I needed a shot of home, and I wanted to run with light blue dusting the sky. Lilac skies are impressive but they always feel just the tiniest bit alien.

Gato was happy to run and gambolled around my legs with obvious joy. He was probably on my list of neglected things, too. Yes, I'd fed him and done the vital things, but we hadn't chatted. And yes, I'm aware he's a dog but he's insanely bright for a canine. Emory says he's remarkable even for a hell hound.

'Sorry I've neglected you,' I said when we arrived home. I patted his head and scruffled his ears. 'I'm getting my head screwed on now, I promise.' Gato gave me a doggy grin and a hopeful bark. His tail wagged his entire body. I kissed him. 'I'm going to shower, and then we'll see if we can find some work to do.'

I sent Emory a text to let him know that I had my mojo back. I got a message back that made me grin.

I hit the shower and washed perfunctorily. I was out in ten minutes and dressed for the day in my usual jeans and a shirt, semi-professional, semi-comfy. I brushed on the barest scrap of makeup; I wasn't in the market to impress anybody, but a girl does like to feel nice.

I opened my work laptop and scrolled through some more emails. Hes had sent me a couple and confirmed that she was on the background check I'd requested earlier. She also flagged up a case on which we were running out of time. She'd done the basic work but now some on-the-ground investigation was needed. We'd been hired to verify if someone called Gerrard Wood was a benefit scammer. He'd been involved in a road-traffic accident two years earlier and had claimed permanent injury. His personal injury claim was ongoing but some Facebook entries had hinted that his injuries might not be as bad as he'd alleged.

I reviewed the work Hes had done. She'd already investigated some of his social media posts. I examined one of the pictures critically; it showed a bunch of lads drinking together. Gerrard Wood was standing, arms round his mates, crutch just in frame in the corner. I could see why the insurance company was digging, but the photo alone wasn't the smoking gun they needed to get out of a pay-out. He could have been leaning on his mates instead of the crutch.

Malingering these days is a big no-no and judged to be 'fundamentally dishonest'. Even if Gerrard had really been hurt in the accident, his claim would be dismissed if he was found to be exaggerating his injuries. He could even be prosecuted. This job had come through an insurance company I worked for regularly; it was a Common realm job but I wasn't going to turn my nose up at it. I needed to pay the bills, no matter which realm I was traipsing through.

Hes had put together a rough itinerary of Gerrard's day. He was a creature of habit; in the morning he'd pop to the shops, and in the afternoon he'd stay in and watch TV. In the evenings he went to the pub. I'd missed his morning trip to the shops, and I was an hour or two off the start of his pub run, so I decided to stake out his house and do some good old binocular detective work.

I fed Gato an early dinner and left him behind. He hates car stakeouts. He stretched out on my bed and gave me a happy wag as I said goodbye.

I drove my little Ford Focus to Gerrard's home in Spital. He was only twenty-three, and the upmarket house was his parents' place. I parked on the street outside and opened an OS map on my dash to give me an excuse for being parked up. Even in the modern age of sat nav, there are plenty of people that distrust technology. Maps never direct you into a river – unless you're really bad at reading them, I guess.

The blinds were drawn, obscuring my view. I checked the time: 4:30 p.m. If he was true to form, my fella would be heading to the pub around 5 p.m. I rang my best friend Lucy while I was waiting.

She answered instantly. 'Jinx, are you okay?' Her voice was concerned, and I felt a flash of guilt. I'd been worrying all my nearest and dearest lately. I'd been a self-absorbed jerk.

'I'm good, Luce, honestly. How are you? How's Esme?'

I could hear the warmth in her voice. 'Esme is awesome, and we're getting on so well.' Esme is Lucy's werewolf. They share Lucy's skin in an odd duality that seems to work well for them. Lucy has greater control over her werewolf than any of the other wolves in the pack because she can *talk* to her wolf. When I'd saved her life, I'd stabbed her with my dagger, Glimmer. You had to be there, but it had made sense at the time. My dagger also imparts magical skills; in Lucy's case, it gave her the gift of piping, as in the Pied Piper. Lucy can talk to animals, including her resident wolf.

'That's great. I'm so glad to hear it,' I said.

'How's Emory?' Lucy asked, a teasing lilt to her tone.

I blushed, knowing what she was inferring. 'He's fine.'

'Only fine? Because I know a guy who can give him pointers…'

My blush deepened. 'Better than fine. He could teach your guy a thing or two. He's two centuries old – he's sharpened all sorts of skills in that time.'

Lucy let out an impressed whistle. 'Girl, you'd better up your game.'

'I know.' I dropped the joking tone. 'I do get a bit worried about it all, particularly the age gap. What if I'm just a passing fancy?'

Lucy snorted. 'Jess, he's proposed to you. That's as far from a passing fancy as you can get.'

'Sure, but I've been a pretty lousy … mate, or whatever you want to call it. I've had my head up my ass.'

'Is it out now?'

'I guess. That stuff with my parents really threw me. But I've been thinking. Bastion said I asked the wrong question. Maybe there's still more to it than I know.'

She sighed. 'I love you, but don't go down the rabbit hole again. It never turns out well.'

'I know, I know. But maybe the question shouldn't have been "who hired him to kill my parents?", maybe it should have been "why?".'

The silence was heavy. 'Maybe,' Lucy said finally. 'Just keep your head. And for God's sake keep Emory in the loop this time about where your head is at. He's been worried. We all have.'

'I'm sorry.'

'You don't need to be sorry, that's what friends are for. We love you. On that note, I need to roll. I'm on security detail to escort wolves needing a recharge in the Common, and it's go-time in five minutes.'

'Are you going to Rosie's?' I asked. Rosie's Café was the nearest portal to the pack's home but its guardian, Roscoe, had recently had a promotion to head of the fire elementals. It was a fairly big deal, though we'd managed to keep it quiet. Emory didn't think it was in my interests to let it be widely known that I'd frozen the former fire elemental leader to death.

I still had nightmares about what I'd done, but at the time it had been justified and I didn't regret it. Benedict had been cruel in the most sadistic and horrifying of ways. He'd needed stopping and I no longer trusted the Connection to do it. Hell, they'd have probably given him a medal. But that didn't mean killing him didn't haunt me at times.

'Yeah, we're heading to Rosie's. Maxwell is running it solo,' Lucy said.

'That must be tough for them.' Maxwell and Roscoe are lovers, but Roscoe would need to be up in Liverpool now he was running the show. I made a mental note to touch base with both of them soon.

'They seem alright. Roscoe visits a lot. I think he misses the days of just being a guardian. I'm sorry, Jess, I've really got to go. Love you.'

'Love you, Luce. Speak soon.'

As I rang off, there was movement in the house and out came Gerrard, carrying a rucksack and leaning heavily on his crutch. I waited until he was a few houses down, slid out of my car and followed him on foot. He was going in the wrong direction; normally he'd be heading to his local, The Stags, but today he was heading the opposite way. Curiosity piqued, I followed discreetly.

Gerrard headed to the train station and I frowned. He

was going off piste. I tracked him, keeping a few paces back. I popped some ear buds into my ears and put the jack into my phone so it looked like I was listening to music. At the station I kept a person between us, but I listened carefully when Gerrard bought his train ticket. He got a return to Liverpool then started hobbling slowly downstairs, carefully using his crutch.

I'd have to keep an eye on him as we entered the city. There are four city stations in Liverpool, and he could get off at any of them. It would be embarrassing to lose him because I wasn't paying enough attention.

I bought the same ticket as he had and passed him on the stairs. Flexi-commuters were heading home and the platform was getting busy. I sat down and watched Gerrard out of the corner of my eye. He sat a few seats over from me, got out his phone and started playing Candy Crush. His crutch rested next to him. So far his movements all confirmed a serious, ongoing injury but … my gut felt like something was off, and my gut is never wrong.

We waited for no more than ten minutes before the yellow Merseyside train rolled in on time. I climbed into the same carriage as Gerrard but sat in front of him. I took out my phone and tilted it so I could make him out in the screen's reflection.

The lady opposite me tried to make conversation, despite the fact I was sending 'I'm clearly not interested' vibes. I gestured to the earbuds, smiled apologetically and focused on my phone again as if I were reading. Thankfully, she got the message.

Talking to strangers on public transport seems odd to me. I was born and raised in the Home Counties where you'd never dream of talking to strangers on a train. The further north you go, the more people speak to you. They call it friendliness, but I wonder if they didn't get the 'Stranger-Danger' message drilled into them when they were kids.

The thirty-minute train journey passed quickly. I kept my attention focused on Gerrard; I didn't need to lose my target because I was wool gathering. We passed James Street and Moorfields stations. As we approached the main station, Lime Street, Gerrard stood up and started to go to the door. He had the crutch out but it didn't look like he was actually putting any weight on it. It would be an arguable point even with a photo or a video, so I didn't bother taking either.

We made our way up to the station forecourt. Suddenly Gerrard cursed, turned around and went back down the escalator. What the hell? He wasn't looking over his shoulder, and he didn't look like he thought he was being followed, but I could only think that he was trying to shake a tail. Weird.

The train station was bustling. I didn't really have an excuse to go back down, but I didn't want to lose him.

Reluctantly I stepped on the escalator and followed him. He was five or six steps ahead of me with no people between us. I hoped I hadn't been memorable enough for him to notice me.

As I was standing there, I realised why he was heading back into the station. His back was bare; he'd left his rucksack on the train. I had my phone in my hand ready to take pictures if necessary, and to give me something to be looking at if Gerrard turned around. I was still near the top of the escalator when someone gave me a hard shove from behind. I flailed for the side rail but the phone meant I couldn't grab it securely.

As I started to plummet towards Gerrard, I let out a very unheroic scream.

CHAPTER 3

G ERRARD HEARD MY scream and dropped his crutch. Whirling around, he caught me and braced us both against falling further. The logical part of my mind that wasn't frozen in fear registered the fact that he definitely wasn't injured; the less logical part of my mind was thrilled that he'd caught me and I wasn't falling to my death.

'Thank you!' I said to him.

He gave an easy smirk as I straightened up. 'No worries, love. Are you okay?'

As I nodded, a man pushed past us and jogged down the remaining steps of the escalator. 'Hey!' I shouted at him. 'You pushed me!'

Predictably there was no answer, he just speeded up. I abandoned Gerrard and started to follow him. He was dark haired, tall and wiry, and was wearing jeans and a black hoodie. He was heading for the exit that opened near St George's Hall. I swore darkly under my breath as he disappeared out of sight around the corner.

I pushed myself harder, panting as I ran. Outside the

station it was rush hour and the crowds had gathered. Darkness was drawing in and my assailant had melted into it. I cursed myself for my lack of exercise these last few weeks; if I'd maintained my usual level of fitness, I'd have caught up to him.

Today was turning out to be a bit of a bust, but I knew something that could turn it around – or should I say someone. I hauled out my phone and texted Emory: *Dinner later? x*

I got an almost instant response: *Definitely. 7:30. I'll bring food.*

When Emory promised to bring food, I never had any idea what to expect. Sometimes he'd arrive with enough take-out for an army, and sometimes he'd have what looked like restaurant dinners in small containers. He liked world cuisine, and I laid a bet with myself that today we'd be eating Indonesian.

It was nearly half-past five, so I had some time to kill before heading home. Roscoe was on my mind after my chat with Lucy and I decided to give him a quick ring. 'Hi, Jinx.' He greeted me warmly, which let me know he was probably alone.

'Hey. I'm in Liverpool, just outside St George's Hall. Are you about?' I asked.

'As it happens, I've just come out of the most tedious meeting. Bar?'

'Sure. I have an hour to kill. Copacabana?'

'Perfect. Give me ten minutes.'

After we rang off, I had a quick debate with myself. It would only take me two minutes to get to the bar, so I decided to go back to speak to Gerrard, if he was still around. I went to the underground ticket desk, and sure enough, there was Gerrard still in the process of reporting his missing rucksack. He smiled in recognition and waved. The guilt nearly crippled me as I returned his smile and tilted my head in the universal 'come here for a minute chat' sign.

He came towards me using his crutch. I looked pointedly at it as he approached. 'You didn't need that when you caught me,' I said.

'Ah, well,' he shrugged. 'It comes and goes.'

'I'm a private investigator. I was hired to find evidence that you're faking your injury.'

His face drained of colour and his mouth dropped open slightly.

'I'll give you a week, then I'll drop the case due to a conflict of interest,' I said. 'They'll hire another investigator. I suggest you use that week to settle your case for what it's really worth. I know this company – if they get any evidence that you're exaggerating your injuries, they'll prosecute you. At best, they'll seek thousands of pounds of costs from you. At worst, they'll try to get you jailed.'

I didn't think it was possible, but Gerrard's face went

even paler. He swallowed hard. 'Thanks,' he said finally.

'Thanks for catching me. Make good choices.' I clapped him on his shoulder and walked away. My moral code is a flexible thing, but that decision had felt right to me. I'd given him his warning and his chance to avoid prosecution, and I hoped he'd take it. If he didn't, it wasn't on me. He'd been in a bad accident and there was no doubt he'd broken his leg; he deserved some compensation, just not as much as he was claiming. I put it to bed. It wasn't my deal.

I set off for the Copacabana. It was weeks since I'd last seen Roscoe and I was looking forward to meeting up. I'd killed his former leader, and Roscoe had been shoved onto the throne almost by default, as he was the closest Level 5 fire elemental. I wasn't sure he was grateful for the promotion from guardian to head of the whole sect. Now he'd have to deal with the Pit, which had been packed by Benedict with his stooges, even though that was against the rules.

It was still early for the Copacabana, but it serviced the business crowd and soon it would be heaving. I glanced around but I couldn't see Roscoe. I made my way to the bar, flashed the barman a friendly grin and ordered a strawberry daiquiri.

My go-to cocktail used to be a pina colada, but now that reminded me of drinking in Alma de Cuba with Stone. I'd been so excited, so thrilled, to be flirting with such a sexy guy; I'd also been so naïve because the whole time he'd been compelling me. The memories of our time together were overshadowed by that one fact that I couldn't quite forget.

I felt a pang of sympathy as I wondered how Stone was. His father, Gilligan, had died only a few short weeks ago. I hadn't got on terribly well with Gilligan, and he'd made it clear that he considered me not good enough for his son; even so, I didn't doubt that the surly man had loved his son.

A tall glass was placed before me with sugar dancing on the rim and decorated with strawberries. I paid up, took a sip and was immediately in cocktail heaven. The chair next to me was pulled out and Roscoe slid in. 'Hey,' he greeted me. 'That looks good.'

'*So* good,' I promised. 'Strawberry daiquiri.'

Roscoe ordered the same then we moved away from the bar seeking some privacy. We slid into a booth next to each other. 'How are things going?' I asked.

'That meeting was dull as hell,' Roscoe complained. 'Stone is such a bore now he's a symposium member. He was a stickler for rules before, but now he's worse.'

I was about to take a sip of my drink but I paused. 'Stone's been promoted to symposium member?'

Roscoe nodded. 'Yeah, he's replaced his father. The circumstances of his father's death have been kept very hush-hush. I never got the impression that Stone was that into politics, and I thought he'd stay an inspector forever, but now he's up to his eyeballs in it.' He hesitated. 'He's been supporting the anti-creature faction. Subtly, but it's there. A vote in their favour here or there.'

I bit my cheek. I didn't want to talk about Stone, and thinking of him throwing in his lot with those who opposed Emory hurt my heart. I didn't want to believe that Stone's change in behaviour might have something to do with me and his perceived rivalry with Emory.

I changed the subject. 'How's it going being head honcho?'

Roscoe let out a small breath. 'It's hard being the guy in charge,' he muttered. 'Especially after Benedict's regime.'

'You need to weed his cronies out of the Pit,' I suggested.

He grinned. 'That was the first thing I did. I made each Pit member take the levels tests in front of all of the assembled elementals. The ones that didn't reach Level 5 got booted out. It was quite a popular move. The Pit is supposed to be sacrosanct, only for the most powerful of us to use as our last defence. If it's stacked full of members from the weaker levels, we'll be perceived as weaker by the other species.'

'So you're smashing it,' I commented positively.

He grimaced. 'Not so much. I was doing alright at first, but I have some quite vocal detractors. There are some that think Benedict's vile methods showed our strength. They think I'm weak.' He sighed. 'I'm just getting the hang of this ruling thing. I think I'll be deposed before I can do any real good.'

I considered the problem. 'You need to do a set-up,' I said finally.

'A what?'

'You need to get someone to help you who's not linked to you. Get them to break some minor rule then come down on them like a tonne of bricks, like Benedict would have done. Can you cast a flame that doesn't hurt the person it targets?'

'Of course. An illusory flame.' He said it as if I should have known that such a thing existed.

'Newbie over here.' I rolled my eyes. 'Get someone to be naughty, cast an illusory flame on them, make them pretend to scream and writhe, and then stop it. Address the whole court and ask them if that's the way they want you to rule? To be Benedict Mark Two? Because in your mind strength doesn't equate with brutality. You contain the most deadly and destructive element, and everyone in the Other respects you. You don't constantly need to yap about your strength like a Jack Russell barking at a big dog. You don't need to prove your strength to the world because the world already fears you. They know you contain the fires of hell and the ability to destroy everything they love. What you need is to get their respect.'

Roscoe was scribbling away on a bar napkin. 'Fires of hell,' he muttered as he wrote.

'Something like that. You don't need to quote me verbatim,' I said, amused.

Roscoe frowned. 'One small problem.'

'What?'

'I don't have any stooges. Everyone knows Maxwell is my partner. I have a couple of other friends, but under Benedict's rule we all kept to ourselves as much as possible. That way there was less chance of a bad word getting back to him and giving him an excuse for a flare party.'

I frowned. 'You see, that's part of the problem. You're supposed to be a community and you're supposed to be a support network for each other. It's hard being different when you're all alone,' I took a long pull of my cocktail and tried to ignore the sympathetic look he threw my way. 'Do you know Samantha Friars?' I asked.

He shook his head. 'Not really. I've seen her at a few gatherings recently, but she's a Level 3, so I haven't had much cause to speak with her yet.'

'She'd help you.'

'Why would she do that?' he asked glumly.

'Well, for one thing she's gay. She was very scared under Benedict's anti-same-sex couples regime. If you made it clear to her that you're quite happy with her partner, I'm sure she'd support you.'

Roscoe gave me a wry smile. 'I'm no hypocrite. Let her love who she loves.'

'She loves a water elemental.'

His jaw dropped. 'Well that's … unusual.'

'Steamy,' I agreed. 'But it's who she loves.'

He nodded slowly. 'It would cause waves if it were widely known.'

'Why should it cause waves? What does it matter what her partner is?'

'There's a fear that if two elementals of opposing elements mate, the resulting child will possess both magics.'

'And that's an issue because?'

'Because the Other realmers – and especially the Connection – wouldn't like it if one elemental could handle more than one element. Why do you think I suppressed the knowledge of your … skills? Any elemental who was present at your showdown with Benedict has been made to swear never to talk about it for fear of losing their magic. Emory arranged the geas himself.'

I blinked. I didn't know that.

'The Connection encourages us to mate within our own species to keep the breeding lines true.'

'To inbreed,' I muttered.

'It's never been an issue for me,' Roscoe said. 'Though Maxwell and I have talked about adopting.'

'Samantha and Bianca could have their own child with IVF.'

Roscoe nodded but still looked uncertain.

'You said Samantha can love who she wants,' I pointed out. 'You didn't say it had to be a fire elemental.'

'She could choose a human, a witch or a seer,' he protested.

'Anything on the human side?'

'Exactly,' he said, missing the sharp edge to my tone. 'The Connection won't have issue with that. And it works both ways. The witches tell us who will be a good match if we want our children to be fire elementals.'

I shook my head in despair. 'And can't you just mate and let your child be who or what it's going to be? Does it have to be driven down a life path before it's even taken a breath? Where is your freedom if the Connection dictates your life partner?'

'You don't get it,' he said finally. 'You haven't been raised Other.'

'No,' I agreed, 'I haven't. I come at it with fresh eyes, and I think some of the stuff you accept as normal is wrong. Anyway, I'm sure Samantha would help you if you'd publicly support her relationship with Bianca. I bet there are others with secret lovers who also don't meet the criteria. Dig them out, support them in their life choices, and you'll be the most popular leader for the last century.'

Roscoe slumped a little in his chair. 'I don't know *how* to be a leader.'

'Luckily for you, I know a man who does.'

CHAPTER 4

I TEXTED EMORY and let him know there'd be a guest for dinner. I got a '*10-4*' back which I assumed meant he was okay with some extra company.

Roscoe was nervous about having a proper tête-à-tête with the Prime of dragons. They'd met Emory only briefly when I'd rescued Emory from Benedict. I assured him Emory would be fine; after all, Roscoe had defended me from the other elementals, and Emory approved of that kind of thing.

Roscoe pointed out that he'd also stood by and done nothing for hours while Benedict had tortured Emory. I winced internally but kept my face calm. I hated the thought of Emory being tortured. We hadn't talked in any depth about the time when he was captured by Benedict. It was something that Emory had suppressed his knowledge of because his own court wouldn't be happy with the knowledge that their Prime had been overwhelmed by another faction. The dragons were another group that was far too obsessed with shows of strength.

Roscoe and I eased the awkwardness by having several more daiquiris in rapid succession before we got the train home. It may not have been the best idea I've ever had, but it seemed a good one at the time. I'm not usually a lightweight but I hadn't eaten and several cocktails on an empty stomach meant I was feeling no pain.

I unlocked the door to my house. Emory was already there and so were Hes and Nate. 'Helloooo,' I called. 'Honey, I'm hoooome.'

Emory looked up and my insides melted. He'd downgraded corporate chic by removing his suit jacket, but he was still in a fitted black shirt that showed off his strong body. His jawline was graced with a shadow of stubble. 'You're pretty,' I said to him in a matter-of-fact tone.

He grinned. 'You're shitfaced.'

I rolled my eyes in response and instantly felt dizzy. 'Nuh-uh. I'm tipsy. I'm fine.' *Lie.* I reached out to support myself with the wall. 'Smartass lie detector,' I muttered.

Emory's smirk grew. 'Good day?' he asked.

'The best!' I agreed. 'Someone is trying to kill me. Isn't that great? I love a good mystery.'

Emory's smile faded sharply. 'Someone is trying to kill you?'

I nodded. 'Don't worry, they're not very good at it. They tried to kill me with a spider in my boot.' I snorted attractively. 'Gato spotted it straight away. And then someone shoved me down an escalator but a nice fraudster caught me. So it's fine.'

Hes brightened. 'Did you get evidence he's malingering?'

I shook my head. 'No, sorry. He might have saved my life, so I warned him and let him go. We'll bounce back the file.'

Hes sighed. 'I worked really hard on that case.'

'Sorry, but you know – karma,' I realised I'd better introduce everyone. 'This is Roscoe, he's head of the fire elementals. He helped us fight Mrs H and Benedict, so he's good people. This is Nate, Hes and Emory.' I gestured to each of them in turn, and they all did the little bow thing. 'I'm starved. What have we got for dinner?'

A Thai banquet was spread out in the dining room. I sat next to Emory, and Hes and Nate sat opposite, with Roscoe at the head of the table. 'I bet Indonesian,' I whispered loudly to Emory.

'Next time,' he promised. He pointedly poured me a pint of water.

I stuck out my tongue. 'I'm not that drunk. I can still feel my face.' I poked myself in the cheek. I couldn't feel it at all. 'Uh-oh,' I said to Emory. 'I *can't* feel my face.'

His lips twitched as he tried to fight a smile and kissed my forehead. 'Eat up and you'll soon feel your face,' he promised.

'You're so wise,' I agreed. 'I think it's the last century of living that's really sharpened you up.'

'Do you think so?' he asked lightly. Through our growing bond, I could feel his amusement and love. He was happy, I was happy. It was nice.

I nodded. 'Yup. That, or hanging out with me.'

'I'd better keep you around then.'

'Sure. So I was thinking, if we got married would I become Mrs Elite? Because that sounds a little arrogant,' I joked.

Emory kissed my forehead again. 'You've been thinking about marrying me?' Happiness was pouring down the bond.

'One day. We're already kind of bonded and we get on well. You're all sexy. What's not to like? So would you ever become Mr Sharp? That's less uppity than Mr Elite.'

'I'm a modern dragon. We could combine,' he suggested with a wink.

I burst out laughing. 'Mr and Mrs Shite?'

Emory barked a laugh. 'Maybe not.' He took my hand under the table, which made eating a little harder but was also pretty nice. We joined in the conversation with the rest of the table and by the end of dinner my buzz had faded slightly. I didn't try the face test again, though, just in case.

We retired to the lounge. Emory passed me a coffee and some paracetamol. I sighed but took both without complaint. I'd probably thank him tomorrow. Besides the eye rolling earlier had made my head spin a little, so they were probably a good idea.

'So,' Roscoe started. 'A vampyr and a dragon in the same room and neither of you are dead. Isn't this the first sign of the apocalypse?'

Emory and Nate exchanged amused glances. 'We try not to mention our species,' Nate admitted drily. 'If we don't mention that we're supposed to be sworn enemies, we get on fine.'

'I like Nathaniel.' Emory said it lightly, like it wasn't a big deal, but everyone knows a dragon only speaks the truth.

Nate met Emory's eyes. 'I like you too, mate. It's damned inconvenient meeting a dragon I like. I *liked* my inbred hatred of other species. I'm going to have to start making my own mind up about things. Damned inconvenient.' Beaming, Hes took his hand and squeezed it.

'Weird,' Roscoe commented again. 'It's like watching the sun come up in the west.'

'Or the sky turning purple or the grass being turquoise,' I pointed out drily.

'Touché.'

I felt like we were getting a little heavy and some lightness was in order, especially while Roscoe and I finished the unpleasant road to sobriety. 'Movie?' I suggested.

They all murmured agreement, and I went into the

kitchen to make some popcorn while they chose a film. I headed on up to my bedroom while the popcorn was in the microwave. Sure enough, Gato was still spread out on my bed.

'Hey, pup,' I greeted him. 'Getting your bedtime in before you're chucked downstairs for the night?' He tap-tapped his tail in affirmation.

'Sorry I had to leave you at home today. It's a good thing I did, though. Someone tried to shove me down an escalator.'

Gato sat up abruptly, looking annoyed.

'I know, rude, right? It's okay, a guy caught me and I'm fine – though the shover got away.' I frowned. 'The spider and the shove weren't the most effective assassination techniques, but we'd best be on our guard.'

Gato nodded and got off the bed, intent on following me downstairs.

'I didn't mean you needed to guard me now. We're just watching a movie downstairs. You relax here.'

Gato fixed me with a gaze that quite clearly said, 'Hell, no.'

I shrugged. 'Suit yourself, but there's only floor space available downstairs. Roscoe is here, and Nate and Hes. Full house. It's kind of nice.' Gato gave another tap of agreement.

'Come on then. Popcorn should be ready.'

They'd picked an action movie that no one had seen

before. It turned out to be cheesy as hell and unintentionally funny, so we spent the night laughing and joking at the movie's expense. After the film Hes and Nate made tracks to her room, and Roscoe excused himself to go to the bathroom. I took advantage of my time alone with Emory to entreat him to talk to Roscoe and give him some pointers about how to be a good leader.

Emory flashed a hundred-watt smile. 'You think I'm a good leader?'

'I know you are.' I gave him a quick kiss and then a slow one. 'I love you. Talk to Roscoe. I'm going up to bed. Wake me if I'm asleep when you come up.'

'Night, Jess. Love you.'

I left him with Roscoe and went up, Gato on my heels. 'Will you chill?' I muttered to him. 'We're home and this house is runed up to the max. Just relax.' He gave me a baleful stare. 'Okay, the spider got in, but that was a one-time deal. Probably.'

I brushed my teeth and prepared for bed. It had been a long day but it had been a good one. Someone was after me; now I just had to work out who.

CHAPTER 5

WHEN I AWOKE, I was alone. Gato was on the floor, and the duvet was pushed back on Emory's side of the bed. I was pleasantly surprised at my lack of hangover. I guessed the food and paracetamol had saved me.

There were sounds of life downstairs so I wandered down. The dining room was laden with breakfast foods and Emory was making a fair dent in the croissants and coffee. 'Hey,' I greeted him. 'You didn't wake me.' My tone was vaguely accusatory.

'I tried. You were flat out and swatted me away.'

'Oh. Sorry.'

Emory stood up and made me a cup of tea. He waited until I was sitting with a bowl of fruit salad before he started to interrogate me. 'So, deadly spider. You didn't mention it was deadly in your text.'

I batted my eyelashes innocently. 'I'd dealt with it by then so there was no need to worry you. The British Arachnological Society came to take it to the zoo. They were really excited. It was my good deed for the day.'

'Rescuing your assassin?'

'It wasn't the little guy's fault someone put him in my footwear.'

Emory frowned. 'I've asked Amber DeLea to come by later today to check the runes. There's a hole somewhere that someone used to slip a spider in the house.'

'It must be a pretty small hole,' I joked.

Emory met my eyes. 'This is serious. Why aren't you upset?'

'I've been in a funk since the whole "my parents arranged their deaths" thing.' Gato let out a low whine and I gave him a reassuring pat. 'But now I have a new mystery to solve.' I trailed off. 'Or maybe a very old one,' I said, frowning suddenly.

'What?'

'You've heard of Faltease? The dude that used Glimmer to try to create new Others from the Common realm?'

Emory nodded. 'Faltease was an asshole. I never liked him.'

I blinked. The fact that Emory might have known Faltease hadn't even occurred to me. Something to dig into another time. I continued with my explanation. 'Someone took it upon themselves to kill the new Others that Faltease created. My parents were among them.'

Emory stilled. 'What?' he repeated.

Suddenly I remembered that telling Emory about my

parents' background, about my own background and my … uniqueness was something I'd been putting off. I'd been different my whole life, a one-of-a-kind lie detector. Then I stumbled on the Other realm, and I had a hallelujah moment where I thought I might fit in, only to discover I was a truth seeker and in a rarer-than-rare sub-species of one. I think subconsciously a part of me didn't want to be different anymore.

I took a sip of calming tea. 'I probably should have mentioned this earlier, but I guess we were always in the middle of defeating Mrs H or drug cartels or stopping the mass murder of all creatures, so it never felt that important. But both of my parents were born in the Common. When they were teenagers, Faltease kidnapped them and stabbed them in the heart with Glimmer. They both survived, and Glimmer made them Other. I don't know what brand of Other they were because they died before they could tell me. Now that seems intentional. You remember when Amber DeLea came here to scry Cathill out of my head?'

Emory nodded.

'You remember you ran in because Nate said I was upset? Amber had told me that someone had killed off all of the Others that Faltease had made. At first it appeared that they'd been in accidents – car crashes, a fall while hiking, drowning after partying too hard, an overdose. Then there was a big fire that killed five of them after a night out. That was when alarm bells started to ring and the remaining victims went into hiding. There were twenty of them and apparently my parents survived the longest.'

'Someone killed your parents for being made Other by Glimmer?'

I shook my head. 'No, that's just it. My parents hired Bastion to kill them.' Now I'd said out loud the thing that had been haunting me these past weeks. 'And it was my fault. I went back in time when I was first introduced into the Other – Gato took me. My parents were meeting with Leo Harfen and I burst in. Mum recognised that I was their future daughter straight away. And I gave the game away because it was clear from my reaction that they'd died and left me. I even told them *when* they died.'

My voice dropped to a whisper and a tear crept down my face. 'I did this to them. I created a self-fulfilling prophecy. They hired the hit because I told them they'd died.' I looked at Emory and my vision swam with tears.

He crossed the distance between us, pulled me up from the chair and into his arms. 'It wasn't your fault,' he said fiercely. 'Whatever you said, they still had a choice to make.'

I nodded against his chest but I didn't believe it. I blamed me. I needed to let out this crushing guilt that had been immobilising me for weeks. I sobbed in Emory's arms until I could sob no more. 'I'm sorry,' I said in a small voice, drawing back and wiping my face. 'It just suddenly got a bit much.'

He kissed my forehead. 'That's what I'm here for. For better, for worse. This is your worse, and we'll see it through together.'

I had a huge lump in my throat but I nodded. Together was a place I hadn't been for so long. It felt good to have some support. Yes, I was Miss Independence if I wanted to be, but I didn't *need* to be.

I had to get back on track because this was too raw. 'The point of all of this is that I was born to two of Faltease's creations. The first time I used Glimmer, I felt that it had some kind of kinship with me. Now I know it identified itself as my grandfather. It had made my parents, who in turn had made me. Glimmer showed me that because I wasn't born of the realm I wasn't subject to all of its rules.

'You remember when we were in the lab and I caught a vision from an inorganic substance? That's why. The usual rules just don't seem to apply. And despite using vast amounts of magic on a number of occasions, I've only been booted out of the Other twice. I don't seem to need to re-charge the same way others on the human side do.' I sighed. 'So I'm a bit of an oddity, even here.'

Emory hugged me. 'You're special,' he corrected.

I gave him a lopsided smile. 'You're biased.'

'I love you.'

'You love me,' I agreed, smiling.

'You think whoever was killing off the rest of Faltease's creations is behind these recent attacks?'

'It's one theory.'

'What's another?'

I hesitated. 'Someone from your court,' I admitted. 'Someone who doesn't want you mated to a nobody like me.'

Emory frowned darkly. 'It's possible,' he agreed. 'But if the threat comes from someone in my court, I'll destroy them.'

'You say the most romantic things,' I cooed.

Emory ignored that. 'I'll dig into my court, and you dig into the Faltease link.'

I nodded. 'Okay. But sooner or later, I'm going to have to meet some of your court. I have resources you don't have,' I pointed out, referring to my lie-detection skills.

'Dragons can't lie,' he argued. 'I can root out the truth as easily as you.'

'I can divine it,' I pointed out. 'One touch and we'll know the truth.'

'If you divine the truth too much, word about what you are will get out. We need to keep you safely under the radar. Let them think you're just a wizard and an empath.'

'I'm not ashamed of what I am.'

'I know you're not and nor am I. But if the Connection finds out, they'll hunt you down and use you.'

'Stone knows what I am,' I pointed out.

Emory ran his hand through his hair in frustration. 'Believe me, I know.'

'Did you know he's been promoted? He's a member of the symposium?'

'Of course.'

'Do you think he's voting anti-creature because of his rivalry with you?'

Emory shook his head. 'No, I think he's trying to honour his father by continuing his work. Grief does weird things to a person. That's Ajay's take on it, anyway, and I trust his judgement.'

Something in me eased. I didn't want to be responsible for Stone's apparent change of heart in any way. 'Can you hit up Ajay for me to see what he can find out about Faltease's twenty? I'll ask Steve Marley, too. I trust Steve, but he's not as senior as Ajay.'

Emory nodded. 'I'll get Ajay on it ASAP.'

'What do you think normal couples talk about over breakfast?' I asked suddenly.

'We're British. The weather.'

I laughed. 'It's certainly mild for the end of February.'

Emory grinned. 'I don't give a shit that we're not normal. We work as a couple, that's all that matters.'

'Yeah,' I agreed. 'We work.'

CHAPTER 6

E MORY LEFT TO go and interrogate his court – subtly, I hoped. I called Steve Marley and asked him to dig into the Faltease files. While I was still on the phone, he tried to access one of them but his security clearance wasn't high enough. Computer said no. I thanked him anyway.

I seriously contemplated hitting up Mo for some hacking, but how could I explain the Connection to him, let alone the files that would be littered with Other lingo. And it was doubtful that he'd be able to access the files. The Other realm has all sorts of protection to stop it being infiltrated by the Common realm.

I'd seen time and again how the Other could protect itself from discovery by the Common realm; it was almost sentient in its ability. I didn't want to embroil Mo any further into this realm if I could avoid it. Bastion had used him to lure me to the hospital when he'd wanted a meeting. That had left Mo feeling vulnerable, and I didn't want to risk hurting him. I put him on the back burner for now in case Ajay didn't come through.

I checked my emails and sent out a few quick replies. I contemplated going into the office, but I rarely had walk-ins, and I could work remotely just as easily. Besides, Amber was coming over to check the runes, and I wanted to see if she could identify a problem.

I put in an hour's work on an identity check for a returning customer's potential new hire. Squeaky clean. I typed the report and hit send, then made a fresh brew and called Lucy for a chat.

'Hey, Jess!' She answered the phone sounding happy.

'Hey, Luce, how are you and Esme?'

'We're good, thanks! We had a great hunt last night. We caught three rabbits.' Her triumphant tone made me chuckle.

'Congrats,' I said. 'Did you share your catch, or eat it all?'

'We ate it all.' Her voice dropped. 'Esme thinks it's best if we keep our skills to ourselves for a while. New wolves – those who've recently turned or been born – can't hunt as easily as we can because they have to wrestle with their human side for control. It usually takes ages for the human and wolf to build a relationship where they can work together synergistically.'

'Esme seems smart,' I commented.

'She is, she's great. Ha! She's preening herself because of your compliment.' There was a pause. 'No, I'm not calling you a bird,' Lucy muttered. 'Other animals preen, too.'

I wasn't sure about that, but I didn't want to get her into trouble with her wolf. I decided a change of subject was in order. 'How are you getting on with Wilf?' I asked.

'Lord Samuel seems fair,' Lucy said. 'Albeit a bit strict.'

Strict? Wilf? Were we talking about the same eccentric dude?

'Apparently, the council is sending someone to investigate him for turning me. It's not made me the most popular wolf in town.'

I winced. 'Sorry,' I mumbled. 'My fault.'

'Yeah, but you saved me from certain doom, so I'll take a bit of bitching. I know bitchiness, I can deal with it. Oh, and I rang my mum and told her I'm coming home from the Hoppas Centre because they've said I'm basically cured. She cried for about ten minutes. So, yeah, it was worth it, Jess.'

Yes. It was worth it.

'How are things with you?' Lucy asked.

I hesitated for too long.

'Spill,' she ordered.

'Someone's trying to kill me,' I confessed.

'What? Why didn't you tell me as soon as you called? Here I am rabbiting on about … rabbits, and you're being gunned down.'

'Spidered down,' I corrected. 'Someone put a deadly spider in my ankle boot.'

There was a pause. 'Well, that's better than being chased by a machete-wielding maniac, I guess.'

'That *would* be scary. Some dude tried to push me down an escalator too, but a good Samaritan caught me so there was no harm done.'

'Anything else?'

'That's it so far but all that was yesterday. The day is young,' I said cheerfully.

She laughed. 'You're enjoying this, aren't you?'

'I've been moping. This was the kick up the ass I needed to remind me I'm still alive and I need to enjoy life. *Tempus fugit. Carpe diem.*'

'Any other useless Latin you want to chuck at me?' Lucy asked drily.

'*Veni, vedi, vici*?'

She snorted. 'That one doesn't apply.'

'That's about the only thing I retained from Latin class,' I admitted.

'We had Latin for five years!'

'Well, I've slept since then.'

Lucy laughed. 'So, you're really okay?'

'I'm fine. I'm going to find out who's trying to kill me and sort them out.'

'You're a girl with a plan.'

'Damn right.'

'Well, if you're all square, Jess, I must go. I've got places to be.'

'A date?' I asked hopefully.

'After the whole incubus debacle, I'm taking a break from the dating scene. Nope, I've promised to do some baking with Mrs Dawes.'

'Are you trying to curb the pack bitchiness with baked goods?'

'You can't be cranky with a cookie in your mouth.'

I laughed. 'A life philosophy that would ultimately make me very fat. I have no self-control.'

'You have some. You're not shagging Emory right now.'

'True. I'm a paragon of virtue.'

She snorted. 'Love you, Jess. Keep yourself safe. I'll be angry if you die.'

'Roger that. Love you, Lucy.'

By the time we finished the call, I'd had a text from Emory. A courier would be here with some files in an hour, and Amber DeLea would be here in two. I felt a frisson of excitement. I hoped the files were from Ajay; if so, he'd come through quickly. I'd owe him one big time.

I had an hour spare. All that talk of cookies reminded me that I'd been eating my fair share of rich foods lately and I needed to keep myself in shape. I whistled to Gato, who was snoozing at my feet. He'd barely left my side since I'd mentioned the attempts to kill me. He takes my health seriously.

'Let's go for a run, pup,' I suggested, and he wagged

his tail in agreement.

I got changed, and we headed out for a swift five kilometres. This time I did it in twenty-six minutes, shaving a whole minute off my previous time. I could feel my body protesting but I ignored it; I needed to be fit.

I warmed down by doing a gentle jog for an extra kilometre. I wasn't far from home when I heard a car engine gunning. I looked over my right shoulder, just in time to see a black Mitsubishi Shogun careening across the grass verge towards me.

I shouted to Gato and we both dived left and kept rolling. Luckily we were running on a path that ran through grass bordered by trees. The Shogun could only get so far before it risked running into one of the oaks – and even a Shogun wouldn't do well in a car-versus-tree confrontation.

I hollered to Gato and we ran out on the other side of the trees, towards home. I risked a glance back and saw the Shogun reversing off the green and continuing straight, as if nothing unusual had happened. 'We're okay,' I panted to Gato. 'He's going.' Despite that, we didn't slow down until we got to my house.

'Well,' I said as we went inside, 'that was a bit of excitement.'

Gato let out a low growl and nudged my phone towards me.

I sighed. 'Alright, I'll text Emory.'

I tried to sound calm: *A car tried to run me over but I'm fine. Safely back home. Catch you later. X*

I got an instant response. *Stay safe. x*

I loved that he trusted me to handle myself. Sometimes even *I* didn't trust me to handle myself, but I liked the vote of confidence. My heart rate was still a little high, but it was nothing that a shower and a cup of tea wouldn't fix. Besides, those files were arriving soon.

I had time to shower, make tea and boot up my computer before there was a knock on the door. I opened the door; it was Greg Manners, one of Emory's brethren.

'Manners,' I said.

'Toots.'

I sighed at the nickname. I'd told him once that if he kept calling me that I'd turn his hair pink and spread rumours about his lack of sexual prowess. I glared at him. 'Have you got the files?'

'Three boxes of them,' he confirmed.

'Great. Bring them in,' I ordered.

He lugged them in box by box. When they were safely inside, I gathered my intention. I wanted Manners hair to turn pink, a bright luminous pink, and I wanted it to stay that way until I turned it back. I released my intention and muttered 'pink' under my breath. I watched with delight as his blond hair changed colour. Sometimes being a wizard is awesome.

Manners left and I stood at the door, watching with

glee as he hopped into his car and checked his reversing mirror. He shifted in his seat and stilled. Bingo.

He looked up and met my eyes and I gave him a finger wave. He grinned at me and gave an approving nod; I was a girl who carried out her threats. Then he reversed off the drive and drove away, pink hair and all.

I was just about to shut the front door when I heard Hes's car turn into my road. I waited for her to park up then called, 'Hey, I thought you had lectures today?'

'Cancelled,' she said, sounding pleased. 'The lecturer is sick.'

'His loss is my gain. I could use some help.' I made Hes a brew and we returned to the dining room where the three boxes were waiting.

'What's in there?' she asked curiously.

'A needle in a haystack,' I said. I explained briefly about Faltease's history. She already knew a little of it, having fallen foul of Glimmer herself.

'So what are we looking for in these files?' she asked.

'I have no idea,' I confessed.

Hes smirked. 'Situation normal, then?'

I stuck out my tongue. 'You take that box and I'll start with this one.'

I opened up the box nearest to me and pulled out a file: Aurora Williams. I settled down and started to read.

CHAPTER 7

THE DINING ROOM looked like a bomb filled with paper had exploded in it. I had numerous files spread out; the one I was currently looking at, about someone called Jake Winters, was full of gory detail. Poor Jake had been in a shop minding his own business when he was attacked with a bottle of acid. His previously handsome face was hideously disfigured. He must have suffered an infection because he succumbed to his wounds when he was in hospital. What a horrible way to go.

The doorbell rang as I finished reading his file. I checked the time; hopefully it was Amber. Because of the spate of trying-to-kill-me events, I checked through the spy hole before I opened the door. Yes, it was Amber. The witch was dressed in her usual flowing skirts and a blue top that set off her warm, auburn hair.

I opened the door. 'Hey,' I greeted her. 'Thanks for coming.'

'The Prime pays well,' she said with a shrug. 'This is a courtesy knock to let you know I'll be out here checking your warding. At first glance there's nothing I can see that's wrong with the rune pattern, so I'll have to examine each inscription individually.'

'Do you need anything?'

'Peace and quiet. And coffee. A coffee would be good.'

'I'll bring one out in a few minutes,' I promised.

She barely acknowledged me as she turned away. She murmured a word and suddenly hundreds of runes appeared on the exterior walls of the house. Emory had clearly gone all out again, as he tended to do in everything.

I went into the kitchen and turned on the kettle. Gato made a whining noise at the front door, demanding to be let out. That was unusual; he usually went out the back.

'You want to go out back?' I suggested but he turned pointedly to the front door. 'Okay, it's your funeral,' I muttered. 'Just don't bother Amber.'

I let him out and shut the front door behind him. I didn't have any blueberry muffins for Amber but I had some fancy biscuits, so I put those on a tray together with a cup of coffee, milk and sugar. 'Hes, can you grab the door?' I asked.

'Sure,' she murmured absentmindedly. She stood up, still clearly engrossed in the file she was reading. She opened the door and I inched out with the tray. As I appeared, Amber fell silent – she'd been talking to Gato.

They both avoided eye contact with me. A lesser girl would get paranoid.

'Coffee,' I said cheerfully, 'and some biscuits.' I set them down on the garden wall and disappeared inside again.

I was about to pick up Jake's file again when Hes cleared her throat. I looked up. 'What's up?'

She bit her lip. 'This is your mum's file, isn't it? You look just like her.'

'Ah. I probably should have mentioned that. My mum and dad were both Faltease's victims.'

'Every file I've looked at, they're all deceased…'

'There were a few attempts to make the deaths look accidental, but by the end whoever was killing them off stopped caring about subtlety.'

'Did you find your mum's body?' Hes asked in a small voice.

I closed my eyes. Despite myself, I saw the horrific scene again. I cleared my throat and opened my eyes. 'Yeah, I did. It was just after my eighteenth birthday.'

Hes swallowed hard. 'I'm so sorry. I knew they'd died, but seeing the pictures… The scene was just so…' She trailed off. 'How horrible for you.'

I shrugged, unwilling to discuss it further. 'So does anything in the files leap out at you? Anything in common between them?'

Hes let me change the subject. 'Nothing jumps out, no.'

'Me neither,' I sighed.

There was a knock at the door, and I opened it. 'I've got something,' Amber declared.

She took me outside and pointed up to my bedroom window. 'There. See that rune there?' She pointed to a wiggly glyph just beneath the windowsill. 'It's been drawn wrongly. The window was the point where the spider got in. If the rune had been drawn correctly, you could have slept with the windows open, and nothing could have bothered you. Because of how it's been drawn, it's ineffectual.' *True.* She was frowning.

'An accident on the part of the witch painting the runes?' I asked, already suspecting the answer.

Amber shook her head slowly. 'No. No accident. The rune has been drawn very carefully to look like the real deal, it's only the last cursive sweep that gives it away. It's a complex rune but it hasn't been drawn inaccurately – it's deliberately wrong. The last sweep is the cancel button for runes. Not even a beginner witch is going to scrawl that accidentally.'

'I thought you did the runes on the house?' I asked evenly.

Amber shook her head vehemently. 'No. The Prime called me but I wasn't available. He wanted it done immediately, so I recommended someone else.'

'Who?'

'Someone I trusted implicitly.'

I noted the past tense. 'Who?' I repeated.

There was a long pause. 'Amelia Jane. She's a witch local to here, very experienced. She might not have been available though, so you'll have to check with the Prime who actually did the work.'

I could tell she didn't believe her half-hearted excuse. She hoped it wasn't Amelia, but she knew Amelia was the likely candidate.

'Can you check the rest of the runes and fix this one?' I asked.

'The rest are fine,' she assured me. 'But I'll need a ladder to fix that one.'

'I'm pretty sure I have one somewhere. I'll find it for you.'

As I went to the kitchen to get the garage door key, I texted Emory: *What's the name of the witch who did the runes on my house? X*

I found the key and went back out. I opened the swing door to the garage; sure enough, there was a ladder at the back. I carried it out to Amber and held it while she climbed up and made the rune safe.

She climbed down. 'All fixed,' she said a tad grimly.

'Thanks.'

My phone beeped. *Amelia Jane. Problem? X*

I showed the text to Amber and she rubbed a hand over her face. 'Shit,' she muttered. Clearly thinking hard, she grabbed her mug and downed her coffee.

I returned the ladder to the garage and went back inside to hang up the key. Amber followed me in to the house with Gato at her heels. She placed her mug by the sink. 'I'll send an invoice,' she said brusquely.

'Sure.' I'd come to expect nothing less from her. She turned as if to go, but then she froze as she caught sight of the files on the dining-room table. She walked into the room as if in a trance and picked up the file I'd left open. Jake Winters.

'I'd almost forgotten,' she said softly to herself. She smiled tenderly at Jake's picture; it was the most warmth I'd ever seen on her face. She blew out a long breath. 'Okay,' she sighed. 'You win.' She put down the file and turned to me. 'Come on,' she said abruptly.

'Where are we going?' I asked.

'To get you some answers.' *True.*

CHAPTER 8

H ES STOOD UP. 'Can I come?'

Amber considered her request. 'Has she signed a non-disclosure agreement?' she asked me. I nodded. 'Do you trust her?'

I nodded again. 'Completely. She was made by Glimmer, too.'

Amber seemed conflicted but finally she sighed again. 'Fine. She can come.'

'Do you want to give me the address and I'll follow you in my car?' I suggested.

'No,' Amber said firmly. 'This is a one-time deal. You come with me.'

As Hes and I slid in, Amber turned to Gato. 'You too.' Gato gave a wolfy grin, climbed into the back with Hester and rested his head on her lap.

I texted Emory: *Amber DeLea is taking me, Hes and Gato somewhere to follow a lead, just FYI. X*

Where? x

No Idea. x

Stay safe. x

I was fairly sure Amber wasn't kidnapping us. She was brusque, at times downright unfriendly, but she'd always seemed to be on the good guys' team. She had hinted she was under a geas, and she had helped stop the virus from being dispersed. So yes, I climbed into her car – but that didn't mean my mum's warnings about Stranger Danger weren't ringing in my ears. Still, Amber hadn't offered me puppies or sweets, so that was a good thing, right?

We drove for an hour before I asked again where we were going. If she was taking us to her place in the Home Counties, we were on a much longer road trip than I'd expected.

'Another half an hour or so,' Amber said. 'Now hush, I'm driving.'

I fell silent again. I checked the road signs and guessed roughly where we were, then texted Emory again: *Shropshire way. x*

He replied straight away: *10-4. I'm tracking your position via your phone. x*

For some people that might have been intrusive, but for me it was just reassuring. I'm a private eye, and I'm used to intruding on others' privacy, so it didn't bother me that Emory would track me to keep me safe. Besides, I'd had too many incidents lately, and it felt good to know someone was in my corner. Particularly someone who was ready to scramble helicopters if anything happened.

I settled in for the rest of the drive. We drove through Church Stretton, a beautiful town set in rolling hills complete with kitsch shops and droves of walkers even in the February chill. Then Amber took us out of the town and down some single track roads. She pulled up to a gated property and entered a pin number. The vast iron gates swung open with a loud, obnoxious beep. No sneaking up here.

We drove up a gravel driveway. The house at the end was a modest three- or four-bedroomed property. It was picturesque, with flowers climbing up some trellis.

Amber stopped the car and turned to us abruptly. 'He'll be able to help you more than I can, but he doesn't know the extent of the damage to his face. Please don't tell him. I've told him that it's not so bad, that he's still roguishly handsome. His looks were so important to him … just don't disillusion him.'

I nodded, now sure of the identity of the person we were here to see.

We climbed out of the car, and Amber unlocked the front door after a brief rhythmic knock, a code of sorts. 'Jake? It's Am. I'm just popping by. I've brought some people for you to meet.'

A voice called out, 'People? You haven't let me have guests in years! Show them in.'

Amber winced a little at his comment. 'For your own safety,' she said, in a tone that suggested she'd said it that many times before.

'Yes,' the voice sighed. 'Safety.'

'He's in the lounge,' Amber said in a low voice. 'Remember, keep your reactions to yourselves.'

I nodded again and followed her. The room was painted a soft duck-egg blue, and the furniture was warm brown leather. Sitting on the sofa, upright and alert, was Jake Winters. The reports I'd seen hadn't shown the true extent of the damage that had been done to him. His eyes were sightless and milky white, and his face had been ravaged by the acid. It was hard to make out the handsome man I'd seen depicted in the file. I shoved back the horror that wanted to rise up in me; the man didn't deserve it, nor would he welcome it.

'Hello, Jake,' I said warmly. 'My name is Jinx and I'm very glad to meet you.' I was. As a Faltease survivor, he was the Holy Grail.

'What's a beautiful girl like you doing with a name like Jinx?' he said with a grin. I raised an eyebrow at Amber who shook her head soundlessly. His milky eyes were blind; he couldn't see me.

'Not so beautiful,' I confessed. 'But the name was born of teenage angst and it stuck. It fits me now. I've got Hester Sorrell with me as well. She's young, still at university, but she's training to be a PI like me.'

'A PI! Well now, I bet you could tell me some stories.'

'I could, but then I'd get sued. I give all of my clients a

confidentiality contract.'

'And what, pray tell, are you investigating that would persuade my darling Amber to bring you to my door?'

'Quite a few things. But just recently someone's been trying to kill me – and I'm wondering if it's because of my connection to Faltease.'

Jake's face was open and curious. He leaned forwards, all joviality gone. 'What is your connection to the foul Faltease?'

'My parents, George and Mary Sharp.'

He sat up, ramrod straight, 'George and Mary? Did they get away, then? Did they hide? Are they alright?' His exuberance was palpable; his words ran into each other, spilling over in his excitement.

'No. I'm sorry. They hid for a time, but … well, it's complicated. They died seven years ago. They were killed by a griffin.'

Jake collapsed back into the chair, deflated. 'Ah,' he said softly. 'You're quite sure? Well then, I'm the last.' He sighed. 'You were right to hide me, Am. You're always right.' But he sounded defeated, and Amber heard it too.

'Jinx has stopped a drug ring and a conspiracy to deploy a deadly virus. She's going to find who's behind killing The Twenty, then you'll be free, too.' *True.* She said it fiercely and with belief. I'd never got a vibe from Amber that she thought much of me, but it meant a surprising amount to hear her vote of confidence.

'And I brought an old friend,' I offered. 'I expect you knew my parents' hell hound, Isaac?'

Jake froze. 'Isaac?'

Gato started forwards and gently, so gently, snuffled Jake's hand.

'Did you do it?' Jake asked softly, wonderingly.

Gato gave a bark in affirmation.

'Oh!' Jake's sightless eyes filled with tears, and he threw his arms around Gato's neck. 'Thank goodness! I was beside myself thinking – thinking—'

Gato let out a sad whine and licked away a tear from Jake's cheek. Jake gave a shaky laugh. 'You're right, of course. Time to turn that frown upside down.'

It made me smile to hear him say that; it was one of my mum's favourite phrases.

Jake dried his tears. 'This has been an emotional roller coaster. I don't often have guests, so perhaps it's a bit much for me these days. I used to be the life and soul of the party, but these days, I only have parties for one.' His laugh was brittle.

Amber's eyes filled with tears but nothing showed in her voice as she replied, 'You're still the light of the room, my love.'

His tension eased and his smile warmed. 'You're somewhat biased. And how could you not be with this handsome mug to love you forever?'

'Exactly,' she agreed. 'I'm lucky.'

He snorted. 'Neither of us is lucky, except in love.' He paused and coughed. 'I've a dry throat. Am, can you make us a lovely brew? One of the loose teas would be great.'

'Of course.' She rose and went out of the room, shutting the door behind her.

'That gives us five minutes, more or less,' Jake said, suddenly matter of fact. 'She won't let me bad-mouth the others, so let's do this quickly. Firstly, I know I'm hideous so there's no need to pretend otherwise. Amber loves to say I'm still the handsome devil I was, but I have hands, and I can feel the marks on my face. Even so, she still loves me. She's tied to me; I'm like a weight around her neck. She can't visit regularly or she'd risk someone finding me. Our moments of joy together are few and far between. Life would have been kinder to us both if I'd died like everyone thinks. Amber doctored my file at the hospital to say that the infections killed me.' His voice was grim. He raised his hand to forestall any empty objections we might offer.

'I live a half-life and so does she. She won't date or marry anyone else. She'll never have the children she once dreamed of, all because of keeping me safe. I've taken her dreams from her, and because of that, I pray with all of my heart that you find the ones behind this and smash them to smithereens. No arrests, no opportunity to play to the crowds. Just itty-bitty pieces. Can you do that?'

'I'm not great at smashing, but I've got a few people who can do itty-bitty pieces if that's what's needed.'

Jake nodded. 'Good enough. I'm tied up in so many geas that I'm in knots, but I can still point you in the right direction. And I think they'd want me to.'

Gato gave his affirmative bark. I didn't quite know what was going on but Gato – or Isaac as Jake knew him – agreed.

'Quickly, then, we don't have much time left. I can't tell you what I *know,* but I can tell you what I *think.* Before my attack, I was hot on the trail of two witches who I was sure were involved – Sky Forbes and Amelia Jane. Amelia is a friend of Amber's, so I never shared my suspicions, and I never found any concrete evidence.

'Sky is something else, however. Amber knows that I've suspected her involvement for years, and she's watched Sky like a hawk, but the bitch hasn't put a foot wrong. Now Sky is the symposium member for the witches. From what Amber has told me, she's hugely powerful now, more than she was in my day. She was always ambitious and ruthless. She hated all things creature, and somehow I think Faltease's victims got rolled into her obsession. She believed that those from the Common who had been *made* Other were an abomination. I'm certain there are more involved than just her, others in the anti-creature movement, but it's all conjecture. I don't have any proof.'

'Leave the proof to me,' I said grimly. 'I've had Sky on my radar for a while now, even though she's been linked to a daemon currently masquerading as Cathill. I assume daemons are definitely creatures.'

'Well now, that's an interesting thing. You see, daemons can't subsume a creature, they can only share a body with one from the human side. Over the years, the creatures have suggested that's because they – the creatures – are somehow holier than the vampyrs, witches, wolves and seers. It's not gone down terribly well. It wouldn't surprise me to learn she's working with a daemon because they're on the human side of the fence too.'

I sighed. 'Of course they are. Nothing in this realm is ever what is seems.'

'A statement to live by,' Jake advised. 'Doubt everything and you might survive.'

The door opened and Amber came in carrying a tray. Jake sniffed. 'Blueberry muffins! My favourite.'

Amber smiled softly. 'I know, my love.' She set the tray down and sugared the tea to Jake's taste before passing it to him.

Jake winked in my direction. 'I'm not sweet enough already – I always need extra sugar.'

'I think you're pretty sweet,' Hes volunteered.

He grinned. 'Well, aren't you the one? You can come again.'

Hes smiled and mumbled a thanks around a mouthful of muffin.

Jake took a noisy slurp, and Amber scolded him on his poor manners. He threw her a wink; he was enjoying getting a rise out of her. 'Faltease,' he said finally, setting his teacup down with surprising accuracy considering he couldn't see the table in front of him. I guessed he knew where everything around him was situated.

'Faltease,' I agreed. 'What can you tell me about him?'

'About the man himself? Not that much. He was widely accepted to be deranged. Much was said about his insanity, and no one noticed that not much of actual value was spoken about him. He was raised in an orphanage in France. He came to England in his teenage years, and he was introduced to the Other. He was a wizard, and his ambition and dedication to his training soon became obvious. He ascended the ranks in the Connection and quickly became an inspector.'

'He was in the Connection?' I asked incredulously.

'Oh yes,' Jake assured me. 'But after his little kidnapping spree, his records were pretty much expunged until only the minimum of information remained about him. He was a black mark to be unnamed and dishonoured so that his name would be lost to time. That was the hope, but there was us – The Twenty. "Faltease's Fallen" the papers called us. But among ourselves we were just The Twenty. Twenty loud and living reminders of the

Connection's failure because they had helped create and carve Faltease into the monster he became.

'We – The Twenty – didn't often speak of the time we were with him. It was harrowing, and many of us had been lost – we should have been The Fifty or The Sixty. He experimented on so many of us, and few of us survived. We believed that he couldn't possibly have been working alone – too many of us were taken in such a short time frame. Once we'd been stabbed by Glimmer, each of us became unique. For example, I'm a wizard, and I can use the IR until the cows come home, but not once have I needed to recharge.'

'Never?' I interrupted.

'Never,' he confirmed. 'I'm a human wizard but I'm not tied to the cycle of portals to keep my magic going. You can imagine that once the Connection learned that, it was experiment and blood sample and experiment and blood sample. All of us, each of The Twenty, turned into something on the human side but with fewer limitations. Your dad was the same, he could heal over and over again and never need a recharge. But if he did something else – for example, if he used the IR in another way – then he'd need a recharge. It was his saving grace. Anytime the inspectors knocked at his door, he just used the IR a few times and eventually he'd be booted out of the Other. It kept them off his case for long enough.'

'If Dad was a healer, why did he become an inspector?'

Jake smirked. 'Well now, he'd been captured with a young lady known as Mary. She was a crusader and she wanted to right wrongs. She'd wanted to be a police officer before she was turned so naturally she turned to the Connection, not knowing the danger that it posed to her and her skillset. And your dad followed.'

'And my mum? What was her skillset?'

'Your mum was something special. She was a truth seeker. The Connection was so excited to have a walking, talking lie detector as one of its own inspectors.'

If I hadn't been sitting, I would have fallen down. She was the same as me, and I'd never once caught her in a lie about it. 'Damn it,' I muttered.

'Ah, you know what a truth seeker is, then?'

I nodded and then realised he couldn't see me. 'Yes. I know.' Perhaps there was something in my tone because he gave me an all-too-knowing look.

'Your mother was all set to investigate our killings – against orders, of course – and then she found out she was pregnant. You were more important than anything else. You changed everything. Your parents had to protect you, and the only way they knew how was to disappear. They consulted a great many tomes hidden in St George's Hall that were accessible only to inspectors, and they came up with a plan. I'm choosing my words carefully here because my oath was worded a certain way. They had friends: a seer, a witch, a wizard, a dragon and a griffin. They trusted us to help them, and we did. I was never sure which of our measures your parents used.'

True.

I couldn't stop the 'huh' that came out. Jake was talking in riddles. Everything he'd said was true, but none of it helped me a jot. Once more I couldn't help but feel like my parents had pulled the rug out from under my feet. They were reaching back from the grave to screw with me.

CHAPTER 9

WE STAYED WITH Jake for another hour, partly because he was a really interesting guy and partly because I felt sorry for him. Nobody except Amber had visited him in who knows how long.

Eventually Amber made a wrap-it-up motion, and I realised we might be intruding on what precious little time they had together. 'Sorry,' I mouthed. I cleared my throat. 'We'd better get going,' I said. 'Amber, can you drop us at the train station in Church Stretton?'

She nodded and stood up. 'Of course. I'll take you now.' She turned to Jake and kissed his forehead. 'I'll be back in twenty minutes.'

'I'll be here,' he said lightly. 'Waiting.' The unspoken 'as always' rang in the room and Amber winced.

'It was lovely meeting you,' Hes said. *True.*

'And you, my dear. Thank you for listening to an old man ramble.'

Hes snorted. 'You're hardly old.'

'Well, some would say I'm still in my prime,' he said flirtatiously, chucking a wink in her general direction, which made her giggle.

'Thank you for everything,' I offered.

He stood and manoeuvred effortlessly around the table. 'I've no doubt that your parents are proud of you,' he said. 'My honour to meet you, Jinx.'

'My honour to meet you,' I responded, feeling a lump in my throat. I touched my hand to my heart and gave him a bow that he couldn't see.

Gato gave a happy noise and moved forwards to Jake, who leaned down to give him a cuddle. 'Dearest of all of my friends,' Jake said. 'I'm so happy to see you again. I have faith that all will be well. You take care.' Gato gave him a long lick on his face that made Jake laugh. 'I finally get that kiss,' he teased. He straightened. 'You've brought me a lot of joy. Thank you for bringing them, Am.'

Amber nodded; there were tears in her eyes once more. When she spoke, her tone was normal. 'No problem.' I realised then that her brusque exterior hid a wealth of emotion that was rigidly controlled and rarely showed.

She said nothing as we piled into the car and drove in silence to the train station. As she pulled up, she turned to me. 'Don't tell me what you discussed while I was making the longest brew ever. What I don't know can't be compelled from me. But … thank you. He seems happier than I've seen him in a long time.'

'Thank you for letting us meet him. I won't stop until

I find out who's behind all this.'

Amber nodded. 'See that you don't. He needs his freedom, the life that he's been denied for so long. I've kept him alive, but I think that now he resents me for it.'

'He loves you,' I countered.

'Sometimes love isn't enough,' she replied bitterly. 'You'd better go. A train will be coming in five minutes. You can make it if you get your tickets quickly.'

I nodded. Hes, Gato and I made a quick exit and jogged hastily to the ticket office. I brought the tickets and we just had time to run to the platform as the train pulled in. The doors slid open and we piled in, the warmth of the train rushing over us. We found a set of four seats, and with a vaguely disgruntled expression, Gato sat on the floor. The rest of the carriage was empty, which was surprising considering it was nearly rush hour.

Hes sighed. 'That was intense. I feel so sorry for both of them. They love each other.'

'It's a shitty situation, but he's alive.' I kept my voice even and tried hard to make sure no bitterness crept in. My parents weren't alive and they should have been. I should have had them in my life until I was sixty and had a husband and grown kids of my own. Jake had been dealt a raw deal but at least he was alive.

'Your mum…' Hes started. 'She was a truth seeker? Like you?'

I started. I hadn't realised Hes had made the connection that I was a truth seeker.

'I kind of figured,' she explained. 'You looked so shocked when Jake told you. And I know you're an empath, so it's not the biggest stretch to reach truth seeker.'

'No, I guess not. Can you keep it to yourself?'

She nodded. 'Of course. I won't tell a soul a thing about today.' *True.* Then she continued, 'You don't fancy being the Connection's tool?'

'No, I don't. The more I learn of the Connection, the less I want anything to do with it.' I frowned as a memory came back to me. 'When I first met the dryad Joyce in Rosie's café, it was clear she was anti-Connection. I didn't know then that she was classified as a creature, and I didn't know about the divide. Stone was selling the Connection as a great world-unifying organisation, with its symposium and the Unity. He painted such a rosy picture and I was pretty excited to believe in it because the Common realm has so many issues. It should have been obvious that the Other realm was too good to be true.'

'So no telling anyone what you are in case this shadowy organisation comes after you. Got it. Your secret is safe with me.' *True.*

'Thanks, Hes.'

'No problem. Now we need to solve the mystery.' She leaned forwards, excitement in every line of her body. 'A seer, a witch, a wizard, a dragon and a griffin. Any ideas who your parents' friends were that they trusted so much?'

'The witch was Amber and the wizard was Jake. The seer? If I had to guess, I'd say it was Mrs H. She lived next door to them and, rightly or wrongly, they trusted her. I know my parents knew a dragon called Audrey who was a friend of Emory's. I've been meaning to talk to her about my parents, but I was in a bit of a funk. As for the griffin, there are two candidates – Shirdal and Bastion.'

'Bastion?' She said in surprise. 'But he killed them.'

I nodded slowly. 'Yes, but at their request. Something else is going on there that we're missing. Shirdal knew my parents and he said he respected them. A friendship with him seems more likely than one with Bastion.'

'Yes,' Hes said slowly, 'but Bastion gave you his last defence potion…'

'Yeah, he did,' I agreed. That had bothered me a lot at the time. Now? It would make a whole lot more sense if he knew my parents better than I suspected.

'What are you going to do?'

'There are a few options. We can investigate Sky and Amelia and do some surveillance. We need to be aware that the people we're speaking to may be subject to a geas, in which case I might be able to divine the truth.'

'Using your mighty truth-seeking powers.'

I rolled my eyes. 'Please don't say it like that. You

make it sound like I'm a superhero.'

Hes grinned at me. 'You can wield fire and water, you're an empath and a truth seeker. You're totally *my* hero.'

I shrugged uncomfortably. 'I'm no one's hero.'

'Someone tried to kill you and you didn't bat an eyelid. When it happened to me, I collapsed into a pile and cried.'

'No, you didn't. Mrs H tried to kill you and you rallied against her. You didn't stop fighting the ropes that bound you. That's heroic in my book.'

Hes blushed but looked pleased. I often forget that she is just eighteen. She's mature for her age and I forget that she's so much younger than me. But she's had her own daemons – literally. Which reminded me…

'We could do with tracking down Cathill, too. He'll certainly know who else is involved. But it will be tricky to trace him with this ever-changing vampyr-age thing he can do.'

'Maybe Amber can suggest something like scrying but with a tracking charm,' Hes suggested.

'Is that a real thing?'

'I have no idea, but it seems like it should be if it isn't already.'

I frowned. 'Maybe we're focusing too much on magic. Cathill has to be using money – maybe we can track him via his credit card.'

'Is that legal?'

I didn't answer the question directly. 'My friend Mo can do it for us.'

She smiled wryly, and I knew she'd caught my omission. I winked and she laughed. 'Okay, back to the griffin mystery. Who are you going to interrogate, Shirdal or Bastion?'

'I wouldn't call it interrogate. I'll ask nicely.'

Hes gave me a dubious glance. 'You're going to ask murderous assassins nicely?'

'When you put it like that, it doesn't sound like my brightest move.'

'We can frame it as "brave", if you like,' she proposed.

Gato snorted. He thought it was a dumb move, too.

CHAPTER 10

THE REST OF the train ride wasn't too bad. The carriage started to fill up so we switched to talking about Hes's studies. She was passionate about psychology, and I could see how much she loved exploring the human condition. Being a PI would give her far greater insight – though not necessarily in a good way. It had made me somewhat cynical at times; it was hard to feel warm and fuzzy about humans when all you saw were scammers and cheaters. Recently, though, I'd seen my share of goodness. People had helped me when they didn't need to and offered their friendship. For the first time in years, I didn't feel alone.

Emory rang when we were ten minutes out of Liverpool and offered us a ride home. I didn't mind the train journey but I *really* enjoyed Emory's cars. He was waiting for us as we rolled into the station. His unobtrusive shadow, Tom, was a few steps behind him, and his much more intrusive pink-haired companion was also in sight. I gave Manners a wave and a grin. He rolled his eyes at me but didn't call me Toots. I counted that as real progress.

We trooped off to find Emory's car of the day. Today it was a huge and ostentatious black Hummer stretch limousine. Gato was excited by it and turned several circles before settling down. Hes asked to be dropped off at Nate's place.

The driver engaged the privacy screen, though it didn't feel particularly private with Tom and Manners riding security detail. However, given that someone kept trying to kill me, it felt prudent not to complain.

We dropped off Hes. While everyone else was discussing the weather, I asked Emory to set up a meeting for me with Shirdal, Bastion and Audrey in whatever order worked. He raised an eyebrow fractionally but nodded.

Pulling out his phone, he texted them all. 'I'll come with you tomorrow,' he offered. 'I've dealt with a few issues today so I deserve a day off with my girlfriend.'

I grinned. 'I'm so lucky. Most guys would hate hanging out while their girlfriend worked.'

'Shopped,' he countered. 'Most guys would hate hanging out while you shopped. I, however, like shopping.'

I nodded. 'I know you do.' Maybe his love of retail therapy came from his childhood when he'd had nothing. Now he had accumulated his wealth, he enjoyed using it – and why not?

We pulled up outside my house and I saw the curtains twitch as my neighbours gawked slightly at the stretch Hummer. I gave them awkward smiles. Tom and Manners went in the house and did a quick sweep. I imagined them shouting 'Clear!' to themselves as they moved around with military efficiency.

Emory sat patiently, clearly used to such measures. I fidgeted and felt awkward, but I didn't complain and I think that gave me brownie points.

Emory's phone pinged. 'Bastion and Shirdal together at your house at midday. Audrey and Cuth later on at their house.'

'That's handy. How do you always organise things so well?'

'I have a PA.'

'A PA?'

'A personal assistant. Summer Lopez. She's one of the brethren. I message her what I want and she sees that it happens.'

I felt an irrational surge of insecurity. Summer knew the minutiae of Emory's life, more than I did. Hell, I hadn't even been introduced to his court. Until recently I hadn't known he was king of several species. I bet Summer had each species noted down and the clan leaders on speed dial. Jealousy wasn't something that came naturally to me, but now it appeared all too easily.

I'd been silent too long. 'What?' Emory asked. 'The bond feels different. I can't work out what you're feeling.'

Simple emotions such as happy and sad seemed to translate fairly easily through our maturing bond, but insecurity and jealousy weren't ones he'd felt from me before. I'd never felt it from him either, but what did he have to be insecure about? He'd lived two centuries, he was handsome and rich. Apart from being a little too controlling at times, he really didn't have many flaws to complain about. I couldn't say any of that about myself.

'Tony Stark marries Peppa Potts,' I said in an apparent non-sequitur.

He blinked and then understanding dawned. We'd watched a few of the Marvel films together, including *Iron Man*, so he got the reference straight away. 'I'm not going to marry Summer. I'm betrothed to you. I love you. I knew Summer way before I met you. If I'd wanted to be with her, I would have been.'

I stared at him flatly. 'Oh really?' Credit to him, he recognised my dangerous tone. He clearly replayed what he'd said and amended his words. 'If she wanted to, I mean. If we both wanted to. But I didn't.'

'Does she?' I asked.

His expression was a little panicked. 'I've got a vibe a time or two that she might be open to the idea, but I've never explored it. Ever.'

Manners knocked once on the Hummer window and opened the passenger door. 'All clear, Prime.'

'Oh, thank God,' Emory muttered, leaving the car as

fast as he could.

I sat a moment longer. Gato let out a huff; he obviously thought I was borrowing trouble, and he probably wasn't wrong. I wrestled with myself for another minute while I gave my insecurity a firm talking-to. 'I'll cut him some slack. It just took me by surprise. I bet she's gorgeous too.' I sighed, then Gato and I edged out of the car.

Manners was still loitering beside the door but Tom was nowhere to be seen. Emory had already gone into the house. Gato peed on a rosebush and headed inside as well.

I paused next to Manners. 'Is Summer pretty?'

'Smoking hot,' he affirmed without missing a beat.

I sighed. 'For fuck's sake.'

His lips twitched. 'She's *really* hot.' He paused long enough for me to get worked up, then he continued. 'And the Prime has never looked at her for one moment the way he looks at you.' *True.*

The hard knot in my chest eased. 'Yeah?'

Manners nodded. 'Yeah. Go get him, Toots.'

I huffed. 'I'm letting that go because you've almost been nice.'

He grinned at me. 'Almost?'

'Where's Tom?'

'Around. He's protection tonight. I'll ride along tomorrow.'

'Okay. Night, Greg.'

'Night, Jinx.'

Manners climbed into the Hummer and it pulled away. I blew out a breath; I'd better go and fix the mess I'd made with my insecurity. Though really, Emory hadn't needed to tell me he could have slept with Summer if he'd wanted to. Men.

'Night, Tom,' I called out to the darkness and I went in, locking the door behind me. I was glad Hes and Nate were otherwise occupied. Emory was hiding out in the lounge, and I let him stew a minute or two longer; it may not have been nice, but it felt justified.

I fed Gato his dinner. 'Make yourself scarce tonight, okay? I need to sort this out.' Gato nuzzled against me and I cuddled him in return. 'Thanks. I needed a hug, pup.' He gave me a big lick and trotted off, checking every room before he headed upstairs to check there as well.

Everyone was taking the death attempts seriously, though I still found them vaguely amusing. I mean, death by spider? Come on. Okay, being almost run down by a car had been a bit scarier, and the threats felt like they were escalating, but I was still struggling to work up any fear. I guessed that after all I'd been through during the last few months, this wasn't even hitting the radar of scary shit.

I put the kettle on to boil and called Mo, my computer expert and go-to hacker. I gave him the all basic details about Cathill that I already had. I omitted the calling him 'Lord' because I wasn't sure if it was a title which translated to the Common realm. Frederick Cathill, currently residing in or around Liverpool. That was all I had – no date of birth, no address.

Mo made annoyed noises but promised he'd get on it. At least the name was fairly unusual, so he was confident he'd be able to dig out the right guy. I asked for an address and confirmation about any financial charges. Mo said that, given the sparse details, he'd have to do some leg work first. I'd already scanned Cathill through all of my legal PI programs and got bupkis. Mo would have to use less legal channels. He promised to update me as soon as he could.

I finished making Emory and myself tea and went in with the mugs and some biscuits. He was on his phone but he set it aside as I walked in. 'Hey,' he greeted me.

'Hey.' I handed him a mug and set the biscuits down on the table between us. 'Sorry about that,' I said finally. 'I should have figured you had a PA. And you're two hundred years old – you've got a dating history. A sizeable one. It's something I'll have to get over.'

'I do have a history,' Emory agreed, 'but Summer isn't a part of that. She's an employee, the same as Tom and Greg.'

'A trusted employee,' I pointed out.

He nodded. 'Yes. She's worked for me for ten years, since I became Prime. I interviewed quite a few people and we clicked.' He winced a little at his poor phrasing. 'We work together well,' he corrected.

I sent him a wry smile. 'It's okay, you don't need to censor yourself. So, you've told Summer about me?'

'Of course. She organised the dinner for tonight.'

'She knows where I live?'

He nodded. 'And your dress size and shoe size. She ordered the shoes and dresses for Ronan's ball. I'm sorry if that's intrusive, I'm just so used to her taking care of everything.'

She knew my dress size. Christ. I made a real effort to get over it. If I wanted to be with Emory – which I did – then this was a part of his life. Having Summer freed up time for us to spend together. Yes, I was going to get over it. Maybe not tonight but soon.

'So what dinner has Summer ordered us?'

'I believe I owe you Indonesian.'

I winked at him. 'Sure. I like things hot and spicy.'

Emory flashed me a mega-watt smile, and I saw him relax. 'Come over here,' he suggested. 'I'll show you hot and spicy.'

I'm no fool, so I did.

CHAPTER 11

W AKING UP NEXT to your soulmate is a nice way to start your day. Emory was still feeling the need to prove his affection for me, and I was woman enough to let him. Let me tell you, that's a gooood way to wake up.

I dressed for a run and was surprised when Emory put on his exercise gear. Gato careened around the house, tail wagging, happy for us all to go for a jog together. I pushed myself and was pleased when I ran five kilometres in twenty-five minutes.

Emory barely broke a sweat; with his vampyric speed, he could have run circles around me. Back at the house we showered together – to save time, of course – and when we were done, breakfast was lain out on the dining-room table. Ordered and organised, no doubt, by the smoking-hot Summer. I was *not* bothered at all by it. Not. At. All.

I asked Emory if he could get me inside St George's Hall to see Sky Forbes because we had time to kill until our afternoon meetings. He texted his Connection spy, Ajay Venn, and a moment later we had a 10 a.m. meeting set up. Strolling into the vipers' nest for a pre-arranged meeting might have seemed like a bad idea at first, but Sky didn't know I was a truth seeker, and she'd feel over-confident in her own territory.

It was time to start putting some pressure on my opponents, and Sky's name had come up too many times for her to be anything but one of those. Besides, I'd have Emory with me, and they couldn't hold him captive without a public outcry. They weren't ready to rock that boat – yet.

I dressed in a suit, more to blend in at St George's Hall than out of any semblance of respect for my meeting with Sky or the office she represented. After we'd eaten a light breakfast, Gato transported me to the Other. As the sky turned purple, I realised it was starting to feel almost normal.

Ronan's covetous behaviour towards my hound was still fresh in my mind so I didn't want to risk taking Gato with me, not into the Connection equivalent of the Houses of Parliament. Thankfully, after a lot of protests, he consented to being left behind. After I'd fed, watered and settled him, Emory and I set off to St George's Hall courtesy of a chauffeur Mercedes-Maybach S Class. My mate may not drive but he sure knows luxury cars.

We were frisked as we passed through security. That struck me as somewhat redundant; I had the IR, and I could summon fire or water at will. That I might be carrying a knife seemed like the least of their worries.

Sky Forbes, head witch and symposium member, had an office on the second floor. Emory and I headed up the stairs without speaking. The halls were busy, full of people in black suits and white shirts. I suppressed the urge to sing the *Men in Black* theme tune. Emory stood out in his all-black attire but he didn't seem fazed; not much fazed Emory for long.

Next to Sky's office was an office with the name 'Zachary Stone, Wizard Symposium Member'. Standing outside, talking with a colleague, was the man himself. He stopped talking when he caught sight of me and dismissed his flunkey. 'Jinx,' he greeted me with a beaming smile. 'You look great.'

I shifted uncomfortably. He was flirting with me even though my mate was right next to me. He ignored Emory, which wasn't a wise move for him politically. Albeit not part of the Connection, Emory is the Prime of the dragons and all creatures. 'You remember the Prime, of course,' I said.

Stone glared but inclined his head. 'Prime,' he said shortly.

'Member Stone,' Emory responded with a similar head tilt. His tone was cool but his gaze was amused; he wasn't threatened by Stone. I felt a surge of irritation. Here was I in knots over sexy Summer, and here was Emory not even batting an eyelid at a man he knew wanted me. Hell, Stone had virtually proposed to me.

Stone shifted his attention back to me. 'Come into my office and we can have a chat.'

It was 9:45 a.m., we had time to spare before our 10 a.m. meeting so why not? Stone might have some beans to spill. I nodded and we trooped into Stone's room. It was spacious and ostentatious, all dark wood and high ceilings. It reminded me of Gilligan's home office.

'I'm sorry I couldn't make your dad's funeral,' I offered a tad lamely, suddenly feeling bad that I hadn't made the time. I'd been lost in my own despair, but it didn't seem right to share that with Stone.

Stone waved it away. 'No problem. You didn't know him well.'

'No. And he didn't particularly like me. He warned me off you,' I admitted.

'Did he?' Stone frowned. 'That sounds about right. He liked to push away anything that made me happy.'

'He loved you,' I asserted, and I wasn't surprised when it buzzed true.

'Yes. He loved me – until he was killed.' *True.*

I bit my lip. 'He killed himself,' I pointed out as gently as I could. Stone seemed to be in denial about that.

Stone smirked. 'After all you've been though, you're still willing to believe the best in everyone. That's one of the things I like about you, Jinx.'

I frowned. 'We found him, Stone. I know what I saw.'

Stone snorted. 'With *Bastion* in the room? Nothing is ever what it seems when Bastion is involved.'

Emory tensed fractionally next to me. What did he know that I didn't?

'What do you mean?' I asked.

Stone went over to a filing cabinet with a very modern locking device. He keyed in a pin number that I couldn't see, a six-digit code, pulled out a file and extracted the front sheet. He handed it to me. There were several pictures of Bastion, both as a man and as a griffin. In a column entitled 'Strengths', it listed a myriad of weapons skills and martial arts. Listed innocuously among all the rest was one line: 'Known Coaxer'.

I hated being ignorant. I looked up from the file. 'Coaxer?' I asked.

'The ability to persuade someone to carry out an action that they have some inclination to do,' Stone explained. 'As long as the intention is there, no matter how deeply buried it is, a coaxer can force it out.'

A chill settled over me. 'You think he coaxed your father into killing himself.'

'I know he did,' Stone said firmly. 'The seed might have been there, but my father would never have committed suicide. Never.'

'No one ever thinks someone will commit suicide,' I said quietly, but the doubt was there now, churning in my gut. Had I been naïve? I tried again to remember what

Bastion had said when we'd found the body. *'I talked to him. He didn't want to be arrested, didn't want to be dishonoured. He chose this path.'*

I frowned. Omission, omission, omission. Would I never learn? Bastion's statement had rung with truth, and I'd accepted it. But had Gilligan chosen his path freely, or had he been coaxed?

I turned to Emory but his face was blank. Too blank. He believed Stone was right, which meant that he'd known immediately that Gilligan's death was not suicide. Outrage welled up inside me, and I struggled to put it aside. This was neither the time nor place for bickering.

'I'll speak to Bastion again,' I found myself saying to Stone.

He smiled. 'Thank you. I know you'll find out the truth.'

I turned to the door but Emory reached out a hand to still me. 'Jinx has been attacked recently. Do you know anything about that?'

Stone frowned. 'Attacked? How?'

'A car tried to run her down yesterday.'

'I'm more than happy to offer you a protective detail,' Stone said. *True.*

Emory snorted. 'You, I presume?'

'Of course. I guarantee no harm will come to her under *my* watch.' *True.*

That got to Emory a little; I saw a tightening of his

jaw that was there and gone in a moment. 'No harm will come to her under *my* watch,' he promised, his voice low and even. When Emory got dangerous, he got quiet.

'I'm perfectly capable of protecting myself, thank you,' I said to the alpha males in the room. 'As my continued survival would suggest,' I added drily.

'Of course.' Stone gave a small bow. 'You're formidable. I doubt whoever is after you will so much as touch you.' *True.*

I touched Emory's shoulder to bring him out of the glare of the stand-off. He followed me out of the room, right in time for our ten o'clock meeting.

CHAPTER 12

S KY FORBES WASN'T what I was expecting. I'd thought she would be young and dynamic like Amber, but she looked like everyone's favourite granny. She was doughy and grey, with a lined face. She conformed to the Connection standard and was dressed in a black skirt suit with pearls around her neck.

Her office was light and airy, in stark contrast to Stone's room next-door. A solitary potted plant sat to one side, wilting and neglected. Her desk was clear of everything except a bell and a clear orb, like a Romany crystal ball. She was being guarded by two Connection detectives, both of whom gave us a cold stare as we entered the room. Sky gave a signal, and they stepped outside.

She greeted us with a warm smile. 'Jessica Sharp and the Prime. Come in, shut the door.' As the door closed the smile dropped off her face. 'I'm sure this meeting will be a waste of all of our time, but young Stone so wanted to see you that I agreed to this farce. You have five minutes.'

I decided to go straight for the jugular and bring up the murder that Reggie had committed by impaling drug-dealing Fred Miller with a tree branch through the heart. 'You doctored a file to make a murder look like a road-traffic accident,' I accused.

'Did I? And why would I do that?' Her expression was condescending. She was unruffled by my accusations – but she didn't ask which murder I was talking about.

'Because you were working with Ronan Fallows.'

'The drug kingpin?' she snorted. 'Well, at least your stories are original.'

'There's only us here. There's no need to lie.'

She laughed. 'I'm not threatened by you. You're nothing, not even a fly worth swatting.'

'I may be nothing, but he is the Prime.' I gestured at Emory.

Sky sneered. 'He is a *creature*. Give a monkey a title and it's still a monkey.' *True*. I hated that she honestly believed that.

Emory ignored her jibe with an ease born of a lifetime of abuse. 'Someone has been trying to kill Jinx. Are you saying that's not you?'

'Goodness, no.' She turned to me with an unpleasant smile. 'If I wanted you dead, you'd be dead. As I said, you're not even a fly worth swatting.' *True*.

My annoyance increased. 'If I'm a bug, I'm the spider in the shower that doesn't go away no matter how many times I get washed down the drain.' Man, I needed to work on my smack talk. I glared at her. 'I stopped your little virus being released,' I pointed out.

'What virus is that, dear?'

I narrowed my eyes, gathering my intention to compel her to tell the truth. Emory must have read the thought in my angry countenance because he stepped forward and touched my shoulder. Her shook his head. Right, I was a *secret* truth seeker. I couldn't go around compelling the people I was trying to hide my skills from. I blew out a breath. 'Tell me about your involvement with the virus.' There was no power behind the question.

She laughed, smirking. 'I think our meeting is at an end.' Sky reached out and dinged her bell. The guards opened the door. 'We're done here. See our guests out of the building.' Her voice was hard and firm; there was nothing doughy about her now.

The guards didn't quite frogmarch us out, but it was close. This time Stone's door remained closed. Sky had only agreed to meet with us so that Stone could 'bump into us'. However, she'd let us know that, which told me she wasn't feeling warm and fuzzy towards Stone despite what Roscoe had said about Stone voting with Sky's anti-creature movement.

We left St George's Hall. 'I thought we could grab brunch,' Emory suggested. 'Ajay said you liked Moose Café.'

I brightened. I love Moose Café, and my fruit salad breakfast had long since disappeared from my stomach. I was a girl that needed to eat. 'Sure, that sound's great.'

'Good, because I made reservations for ten-thirty.'

I bit back the comment that *Summer* had made the reservation and felt like a slightly better person for doing so. 'Great,' I responded.

We started towards Dale Street. We left the gardens and ducked down Victoria Street, holding hands and moseying. If it hadn't been for the meeting with Mrs Bitch, it would have been romantic. We turned onto Cumberland Street – and that's when things got funky.

The vibrations started in the soles of my feet. 'Er,' I said eloquently to Emory, 'do you feel that? Does Liverpool have earthquakes I don't know about?'

'Not as far as I know, but it certainly feels like it. Let's get out of this street – quickly.' Emory was right: we needed to leave. Cumberland Street was narrow, no more than eight metres at its widest, and I didn't fancy being stuck here if the masonry started tumbling.

We picked up the pace as the vibrations increased significantly. Emory reached out a hand to steady me. That was when a giant worm erupted from the ground in a spray of tarmac and rubble. 'Holy shit,' I swore. 'What the hell is that?'

Emory seemed similarly taken aback.

The worm, if you could call it that, was gargantuan. It

filled the street with its gaping maw and reared up towards the sky. Its mouth was full of razor-sharp teeth that were half the size of me, and there was a spray of spikes around its mouth not dissimilar to Gato's. Its eyes were translucent and I couldn't tell where it was looking.

The beast let out an earth-shattering roar that seemed at odds with its pale-pink skin. A worm shouldn't make that noise, no matter the size of it. God, it was huge. It filled the whole of Cumberland Street, almost scraping both sides of the buildings.

'What is it?' I asked Emory again.

'An ouroboros,' he said grimly.

'It's not eating itself,' I quipped.

'No, it doesn't really do that.'

'Of course not. That would be too easy.'

The worm turned and slammed down its head to-wards us. We leapt back, barely missing becoming worm food. It straightened up and towered above us once more.

'It's a creature,' I whispered. 'That means it's one of yours, right?'

'Not every creature is mine,' Emory whispered back.

'Well, how am I to know which is or isn't yours? You haven't shown me your terms and conditions for being the king of the creatures.'

'If it's attacking me, it's not one of mine,' he said flatly and entirely too loudly.

The worm struck down towards us again, and the

ground shuddered and shook with the impact.

'It could be one of yours, but rogue,' I suggested.

'It's not mine,' he hissed. 'Do we have to discuss this right now?'

'Are you sure you can't just order it? Why don't you dragon up and talk to him. You know, wyrm to worm?'

'You think you're funny, don't you?'

'Hilarious,' I grinned back unrepentantly.

Emory rolled his eyes and gestured for me to back up quietly. I edged back and gave him the thumbs up. He cleared his throat. 'Lambton Worm, I am the Prime Elite—' That was as far as he got before the ouroboros tried to hit him again, pounding yet more tarmac into oblivion.

'We need to scare it,' Emory whispered. 'If the old tales are true, it doesn't like fire. This behaviour isn't what I'd expect of it. Try to scare it – we mustn't burn it unless we have to. Something is going on here.'

Something else is *always* going on; it's the Other realm's tag line. Nothing is ever as it seems.

I concentrated on imagining fire, a lot of fire, fire that wouldn't burn Emory or I but would look the part. I imagined a sheet of dancing fire, and it appeared before me, all of three-feet tall.

Emory laughed. 'A little bigger,' he suggested.

'That's what she said,' I responded, quoting the old joke.

'As long as it's not what *you* said,' he quipped.

I felt myself blush. Nope, I hadn't any complaints.

Emory's hands were crackling with giant fireballs. He threw them up towards the worm but let them hover near it. His fire wasn't illusory; his fire would burn.

The worm felt the heat, screamed and reared back, but it wasn't scared enough to leave. I cast my sheet of fire bigger and higher. As it grew, the flames danced on the street and on the buildings. The graffiti-ridden walls blackened but the ouroboros stayed put.

'We have to hurt it,' I said regretfully to Emory.

He nodded reluctantly. One of his fireballs moved forwards, striking it in the neck. It screamed and the smell of burnt flesh filled the air. I choked on the acrid scent and my eyes watered, but still the worm didn't go. Its determination defied logic.

It dived forwards blindly, and I let the flames and spread and dart up to it. I hoped it would feel the heat and retreat, but it didn't. Grimly, I moved my sheet of flame forwards still further and scorched its body. Its screams rent the air, but finally it pulled back then disappeared back into the earth. I held the flames in place a moment longer before letting them fall.

'We have to go,' Emory urged.

'But what about this mess?'

'The Connection will clear it up. It's about all they're good for. But we don't want to be stuck here when they come.'

'Red tape and paperwork?'

'And the risk of them deciding its best to try to wipe our minds,' he said grimly.

We picked up the pace as we retreated back into Victoria Street. Emory tugged me onto Mathew Street, where we mingled with the crowds looking at the Cavern Club and the Beatles' statues.

I sighed. 'We're not going for brunch any more, are we?'

'Not at Moose,' Emory confirmed. 'Someone knew our movements well enough to set an ouroboros on us in the middle of Liverpool. I'm not keeping our reservation.'

It made sense but I was still disappointed; I'd been looking forward to a Mighty Moose. 'It could be a coincidence,' I said hopefully. 'Just a random place he popped up. You know, wrong place, wrong time?'

Emory wrapped an arm around my shoulders and gave me a reassuring squeeze. 'She. It was a female. Maybe it was random, maybe not. I grant you this is the most bizarre mode of death threat yet, but I'm not willing to risk you by calling it coincidence. I've messaged Manners to pick us up in fifteen minutes near China-town.'

Up ahead some inspectors were pushing their way through the crowds. I figured we didn't want an extended chat with them, so I pulled Emory close to me and kissed him. We leaned against the wall, kissing in a truly revolting public display of affection, which I thoroughly enjoyed. Even near death didn't lessen Emory's appeal.

We kissed quite a bit longer than necessary. When we finally pulled apart, the men in black had long since gone past us. We separated reluctantly and walked briskly through town until we saw the red-and-gold arches of Chinatown.

Manners was outside the Mercedes-Maybach, tension in every line of his body. He scanned us and relaxed fractionally, then opened the door and said something to the driver. We all hustled in. Manners sat next to the chauffeur and the car moved off at a leisurely pace like we weren't fleeing a crime scene.

Calm, cool, criminal.

CHAPTER 13

M Y TUMMY RUMBLED loudly. With an amused glance, Emory directed the chauffeur to take us to the McDonald's drive-through on the Croft Retail Park. I could have kissed him. So I did.

Now the danger was passed, and once I was happily fed on chicken nuggets, Emory relaxed again.

'We have the best dates,' I commented.

He flashed me a grin. 'Life's never boring with you.'

'I aim to please. Now, tell me about this Lambton Worm.'

'It's from County Durham originally, or so the tales go.'

'We're miles from Durham so it's a very well-travelled worm,' I commented. 'Do you think it was lost? Maybe it doesn't like stopping for directions.'

'I think it was sent here on purpose.'

'For what reason?'

'To kill you,' he said firmly. 'And to be clear, I'm not leaving your side until we sort out who is behind these attacks on you.'

'That's nice and romantic and all, but what if it takes weeks? You have a kingdom to run. Several kingdoms.'

'This is the modern age. I can do video calls.'

'With dragons who don't even accept telephones yet?' I said dubiously.

'The brethren can organise it. All the supplicant has to do is turn up. It will be fine. Remote hearings – it'll be a thing before we know it. You've got to ride the wave.'

I grinned at that. 'Well, for now you can ride shotgun. If this carries on more than a week we can re-evaluate. Deal?'

'Deal,' Emory agreed easily.

'Did you notice the graffiti on Cumberland Street?' I asked.

'I was a bit distracted by the giant murderous ouroboros,' he commented drily.

'It said "Kill all the creatures".' I fell silent.

He picked up my hand. 'I forget sometimes that you're new to all of this. You know the anti-creature movement is out there.'

'Yeah. But I suppose I thought they just wanted you as second-class citizens, not wiped out.'

'Remember the deadly airborne virus that would have killed all creatures?'

I winced. 'Yeah, but I thought that was an extremist outliers' view.'

He shook his head. 'No, the anti-creature movement

wants to hunt us down, like shooting a lion on the African plain or fox hunting across the British hills. They think it's sport because we're animals.'

'But you're not animals – you're all sentient.'

'Is it alright to kill the selkies or the unicorns or the ouroboros then?'

'No! Of course not. I mean, I'm against hunting anyway. I'm an animal lover. I do get hunting for food, that's different, but hunting for sport – no.'

'Funnily enough, in the years since its inception the Connection has been responsible for stamping down a lot of the anti-creature movement. But recently, at least since I've been Prime, the winds have shifted. That prejudice seems present even in the inspector training, or so Ajay tells me.'

I shook my head. 'That's just wrong.'

'It's a shame, but we play with the cards that are dealt to us. Hopefully the sentiment will fall out of fashion again.'

The car came to a stop outside my house. We were early to meet with Shirdal and Bastion. I opened the door and went into the lounge, looking for Gato. Instead I found Hes and Nate in *flagrante delicto* on my sofa.

'Oh my goodness!' I said, whirling around and covering my eyes. 'Erm, sorry.' I stepped out of the room and rushed for the kitchen.

Emory was grinning. 'I'm going to buy you a new

sofa,' he offered.

I opened my mouth to protest and closed it with a snap. I couldn't unsee what I'd seen. Nate could have the sofa and he and Hes could re-enact happy times. Really happy times.

'Good for them,' Emory continued. 'Some vampyrs are so traditional they don't get much past missionary.'

'And you'd know that how?' I asked archly.

'Well, to be honest it's a common joke. But I can now say that it's a false rumour.' He was chuckling, obviously finding it all hilarious.

'I can't unsee that,' I complained.

'I'll show you some stuff later that will blow it out of your mind,' he promised with a wink.

I felt myself smile. 'Promises, promises.'

Hes burst in the kitchen. 'I'm so sorry.' She was wringing her hands. 'Nate's roommate was just being so annoying, and my dorm had a fire alarm and we couldn't be bothered waiting, so we thought we'd pop back here. Your diary said you had a twelve o'clock meeting and an afternoon meeting.'

I nodded. 'Next time I'll put the location of the meeting in, too,' I promised. 'The twelve o'clock is here.'

'I'm so sorry.' Hes was mortified. Her skin was fuchsia pink.

I held up my hands to forestall her. 'Honestly, it's fine. If I'd been paying attention, I would have noticed that Nate was close and he was … well.' My cheeks warmed too. 'I said use my house as your own and I meant it. But next time maybe put the chain on the front door so I don't see it,' I suggested.

'Chain,' Hes repeated dumbly. 'Right. That would have been a good idea.'

I cleared my throat. 'Anyway, the meeting is in half an hour. I'm just going to check on Gato.'

'Gato's here?' Hes said incredulously.

'Mm. I left him here for the morning.'

Hes couldn't get any redder. 'Poor Gato. He's been hiding away all this time. Nate and I will take him for a nice long walk to make up for it.'

'Sure, if he wants to go.'

'We'll go to the beach,' she suggested.

'He does love the beach,' I agreed.

I opened the kitchen door and whistled for Gato. He came trotting down from my bedroom and gave Hes a doggy grin, his tongue lolling.

'Oh God,' Hes said, horrified. 'He knows what we were doing.'

'We weren't terribly quiet,' Nate said as he came in. 'Sorry about that,' he said to me. 'I normally notice you getting closer but I was somewhat distracted.'

'No worries.' I smiled at him. I could feel his happiness now that I hadn't got our connection tamped down. It was nice, and I was pleased for him.

'We're going to take Gato for a walk,' Hes blurted

out. 'To the beach. To make up for keeping him pinned down in the bedroom.'

Gato was definitely grinning. 'You want to go to the beach?' I asked him. 'I'm staying in the house with Emory so you're good to go.'

Gato gave an affirmative bark and spun round in excitement.

'He wants to go,' I confirmed.

'Right. Well. We'll just ... go,' Hes muttered awkwardly. She gave us a wave and grabbed Gato's lead, just for appearances' sake.

When they were gone, I turned to Emory. 'I think I'd quite happily let the Connection wipe my mind now, as long as they included up to this moment.'

He laughed. 'It's not that bad. But how do you like this?' He held up a picture of grey sofa with a pale wooden frame.

I shrugged. 'I'm not really into interior design.' I looked at the mish-mash of things around me. 'As you can see. Whatever works for you is good with me. Nothing neon.'

'Nothing neon,' he repeated. 'That's an easy rule to keep to.'

'That's me, Miss Easy-To-Live-With.'

'You are,' he agreed. 'That's how you ended up with two occasional roommates.'

'You think I should be mean and they'll go away?'

'No, I don't think they would. They love you too.'

CHAPTER 14

T HERE WAS A brisk knock on the door. 'Manners,' Emory confirmed. 'I expect the griffins are here.'

I started to rise to go to the door but he stopped me. 'I'll get it, just in case,' I bit back my protests with some effort. All of this protection detail was wearing very thin, very rapidly. I was used to being independent.

I reminded myself it was because Emory loved me, and I did some of the breathing exercises that Dad had taught me. My frustration was locked up tight when Shirdal and Bastion joined us. Emory took the seat next to me, and Shirdal and Bastion sat on the sex sofa. If I hadn't been so tense, it would have been funny.

'We need to get something out of the way first,' I said, thinking of my promise to Stone. I met Bastion's cold eyes. 'Did you kill Gilligan Stone?' I asked.

Not a single flicker of emotion crossed Bastion's blank face. 'He killed himself,' he responded. *True.*

'Did you coax him to kill himself?' I asked, almost afraid of his answer.

'Yes,' he replied evenly.

'Damnit, Bastion! He should have faced justice, gone to trial.'

Bastion's hard eyes met mine. 'Grow up, Jessica Sharp. There is no justice here. This isn't the Common realm with your judge and juries. The Other just has executioners, and I'm one of them. He poisoned my daughter. I couldn't leave that unanswered even if I'd wanted to. I'd be judged weak, and weak equates to dead in my line of work.'

'Stone wasn't anti-creature before this, but now...'

Bastion snorted. 'He may not have attended rallies and sprayed slogans on buildings, but he was anti-creature. Perhaps he hadn't admitted it even to himself, but you only need to look at his record of dealing with the creatures to know that he despises them. For every human head that rolled, there were four creatures that faced the same fate. I'm an assassin, but I accept what I am. Stone's an assassin with a badge saying he is sworn to protect.'

I wanted to protest but I didn't know the facts and figures; maybe they did speak for themselves. All I knew was I'd seen Stone behead a vampyr without hesitation, plus he'd told me the story of the water elemental that he'd killed. He hadn't told me anything about killing creatures – but that didn't mean he hadn't. After all, he'd called himself the bogeyman.

I shook my head a little to clear it. 'Enough about

Stone. That's not why I asked you both here.'

'Ordered,' Bastion corrected, lounging back insolently on the sex sofa. It made me smirk a little. He caught my expression and raised an eyebrow. I sniggered. The deathly scary assassin was probably sitting on a wet spot. Petty, I know, but funny.

I turned to Shirdal. 'You knew my parents.'

'Yes, sweetheart, I knew them. They arrested me once.' He threw me a wink. 'Couldn't blame them, though. They were very eager and by the book. They frowned on torture, maiming and death. You're a lot more fun.' *True.*

I glared. 'I frown on torture, maiming and death.'

He grinned. 'Maybe, sweetheart, but it follows you and Azhdar here around like a lost puppy.'

I wanted to argue but I guessed that technically we might have maimed the ouroboros a little with our fires so I didn't. 'Would you call my parents your friends?' I asked.

Shirdal blinked. 'Er, no offence, Jessica Sharp, but no. We weren't bosom buddies, though I did flirt with your mum on occasion.'

Eww. I ignored that and turned to Bastion. 'You were friends with them,' I asserted.

He looked at me for a long moment before inclining his head in a fractional movement I might have otherwise missed.

My heart started to beat faster. 'You helped them,' I said.

He nodded again and this time it was clear for all to see. His eyes were curious now, waiting to see what I knew, giving away nothing.

'They were your friends and you helped them. You performed a rite with some others,' I continued.

'To what end?' he asked calmly.

I slumped down. 'I don't know,' I admittedly glumly. 'You did a rite that helped them hide.'

'The rite was to do more than that,' Bastion hinted.

'What else?' I asked desperately.

'I'm under a geas. Even if I wanted to tell you, I can't.'

'I could divine it,' I said desperately. I let the ocean recede and started to prepare myself. Emory's love beat like a steady drum in the room, Shirdal's curiosity hummed – and Bastion? Bastion was silent as the grave.

'You could try,' Bastion agreed. 'But your parents knew what you might be. The geas on me is strong, stronger even than your divination. To break it might kill you – or me. For now, I cannot give you the answers you seek.'

'Cannot, or will not?'

'Cannot,' he repeated firmly. 'But there is one who can.'

'Who?'

He nodded to Emory. 'Seek out one of his.'

'Audrey,' I breathed.

An almost-smile touched Bastion's lips. Bingo.

'Thank you,' I said gratefully. Without thinking, I flung myself into his arms to give him a hug. He stiffened and I started to apologise, suddenly realising he might think I was trying to divine him, but the apology stuttered and died in my throat as his hand touched mine. I felt it then, a fierce protective affection, loud and roaring. He cared about me. He had protected me; he would continue to protect me from everything that he could.

I drew back, looking at him with wonder. 'Oh,' I said in a voice inches from tears, 'I didn't know.'

Bastion drew me back into the hug. I knew, as he did it, that it was the first embrace he'd experienced since my mother had died. I hugged him back fiercely. We stayed like that for a long minute before he gave me one last squeeze and shifted back, his face as granite as ever. But I *knew*. I had felt it. He cared for me, like a godfather or favourite uncle. He was fiercely protective of me, he would *die* for me – and I had treated him like utter shit. And damn it, he'd killed my parents at their request because he had loved them too. I'd treated him like a villain, and he'd been the misunderstood hero this whole time.

'I'm so sorry,' I breathed, tears welling again.

He brushed them away with his fingers. 'It is done,'

he said simply.

I nodded. Shoulda, woulda, coulda. We couldn't live in the past, haunted by regrets, we could only move forwards.

I closed my eyes and visualised the calm of the sea rushing into the beach and washing away my emotions. Level headed once more, I opened my eyes to meet Bastion's. I had a mystery to solve and a dragon to visit, and there was no time like the present.

CHAPTER 15

S HIRDAL AND BASTION made tracks, or perhaps they took wing. All I know is that they left and they had no car.

'Fill me in on the blanks?' Emory asked.

'Sure,' I frowned. 'Did I mention my mum was a truth seeker?'

'No, that may have slipped your mind.' He said it mildly, but I felt the reproof. He kept discovering secrets that I hadn't meant to keep.

'I only found out yesterday,' I explained apologetically. 'You distracted me with the hot and spicy … Indonesian food.'

He grinned. 'I'll forgive you then.'

'Right. So she was a truth seeker like me. She kept it hidden all those years. All those times I complained about being different, she never once said she was like me, nor did she ever lie to me. She must have been a master wordsmith to never ping my radar.'

'She wanted you to know she'd never lie to you.'

'She omitted a helluva lot.'

'Maybe, but to protect you. I can get on board with that.'

'You're not the one fumbling in the dark,' I muttered.

'I like fumbling in the dark,' he said, trying to lighten the mood.

'My mum and dad were friends with Bastion. I don't know exactly how their friendship came about, but they asked him to watch over me. He feels … like an uncle. He loves me. He wants to protect me.'

Emory sighed. 'All that energy I expended threatening him, and he's your guardian angel.'

I smiled at the image; there was nothing angelic about Bastion. 'Something like that,' I agreed.

Emory checked the time. 'Why don't we go to Audrey's?' he suggested. 'We won't be too early.'

'Yes,' I agreed, suddenly feeling itchy. 'Let's go.'

Not too long before, Emory had given me a Mercedes. I'd protested a little at the time, but the truth is that I loved that car. It was so comfy and such a dream to drive. I'm a petrolhead at the best of times and it made me genuinely happy to hop behind its wheel.

Emory hadn't found time in the last two hundred years to learn to drive, so he climbed into the passenger seat. Gato was still out with Nate and Hes, and the car felt a little empty without him turning three times in the boot.

We drove for about an hour. Emory directed me

when I needed him to but I remembered much of the route. We left the Wirral and went into rural Liverpool. Eventually we parked up by the lake, and Emory and I walked hand in hand through the woods to the glass mansion nestled in the trees. Audrey's home was a modern-looking building, all glass and wooden cladding. Today the occupants were sitting in the living room, playing Scrabble.

They beamed as we approached and Cuthbert rose to open the door. 'Prime, my boy!' he greeted Emory warmly. 'Come on in. Jessica, you're looking very well. Lovely to see you both.' He stepped back and held the door open.

Emory went in first, kicking off his shoes and placing them by the door. I went into the broiling heat and quickly shrugged off my jacket. I started to take off my shoes and paused, raising an eyebrow at Cuth.

'Go ahead and remove them,' he advised. 'There's no more time-travel in your future that I know about.'

'Small mercies,' I muttered, removing my shoes and placing them by Emory's much fancier brogues.

The last time I'd seen Audrey and Cuthbert they had been ill, laid low by a virus that someone had injected into Audrey when she was unaware. She'd collapsed a day or two later and Cuthbert, as her mate, had been similarly afflicted. We'd found them the antidote in time, but I could still vividly recall their fragility. They had both lived centuries and had reached the age where their bodies showed it. Cuthbert's back was bowed with age, and he moved with slow, shuffling steps. Despite that, his eyes were sharp and clear, as was his mind.

Emory was ahead of me. He'd already shucked off his suit jacket and was kneeling at Audrey's feet. 'Prime,' he greeted her respectfully.

'Prime Elite,' she countered, greeting him in turn. 'I won't be kneeling, dear boy. My knees just wouldn't take it.'

Emory flashed her a grin. 'No need to kneel to me, Audrey.'

'And that's how I feel about you so up you get, Emory. Sit beside an old dragon and take some tea.'

There was a brightly coloured teapot on a tray and four mugs. Emory poured some for me, added just the right amount of milk and passed it to me.

I settled on the sofa opposite Audrey, and Cuthbert joined me. 'You're looking so much better,' I commented to them both. 'It's good to see.'

Cuthbert smirked. 'It'll take more than a deadly virus to lay my Audrey low. She invented the word "formidable".'

Audrey smiled at him indulgently. 'The virus was bad enough. Let's not encourage further attempts.' She sipped her tea and looked at me. Her hair was braided and drawn back from her face in a bun, and her expression was a little stern. 'I expected to see you sooner,' she commented.

I felt myself flush slightly. 'I've been having a temper tantrum,' I admitted. 'I'm over it now.' I took a deep breath. This could be the moment that I finally learned the truth. 'Can you answer some questions for me? I know that you were friends with my parents because I saw a picture once of you all together. A sneaky elf wiped my mind, so it's taken me a while to come banging on your door. But … you knew them? You were friends?'

Audrey nodded. 'Yes, good friends. And you know your parents, they're thorough people. A lot of what I know is locked up with a tightly worded geas that I can't break.'

'Amber DeLea,' I huffed.

'She's a very strong witch,' Cuthbert interjected. 'She's touted to be the next symposium member once Sky's term is done.'

I pictured the doughy bitch woman I'd met. 'I bet Sky just loves that.' I sighed. 'So the geas has you locked up tighter than Houdini in a fish tank. Why did Bastion point me in your direction if you're no more able to talk to me than he is?'

Audrey smirked. 'Because your parents are clever, but they weren't born to the Other realm. They overlooked one small thing.'

Hope flared in my chest. I leaned forwards, desperately trying to control the sudden excitement thrumming through me. 'What thing?'

'We're mated,' Cuthbert continued seamlessly. 'And your parents didn't place the geas on me.'

'Holy fuck,' I swore, heart thudding. 'You know what's going on, the truth, and you can talk?'

Cuth nodded slowly. 'I can talk,' he confirmed but his expression was serious, as if he wasn't sure he should reveal what he knew. He looked at Audrey but she was nodding at him too.

'If you know something,' Emory started, 'you have to tell us. Jinx can't be kept in the dark any longer. Someone is trying to kill her. She's being targeted, just like her parents were targeted. We're hamstrung without knowing what dark secrets you're hiding.' His tone was a mite accusatory.

I felt obliged to defend Audrey and Cuthbert. 'Keeping it to themselves really wasn't their choice,' I pointed out. 'They're respecting my parents' wishes and the damn geas.'

Cuthbert agreed, his eyes sombre. 'Yes. And keeping you safe was always your parents' sole focus. They loved you. They thought that if they were dead, you wouldn't be targeted. They knew you'd find the Other realm because you'd had a trip into the Third realm, but they hoped you'd keep a discreet presence.'

I grimaced a little at that. My parents had hammered

into me that I should stay off the radar, that the wrong people would use my skills and keep me hostage. Despite that, I'd told a great many people what I was. I'd been excited to have a label, and maybe just a little naïve. I'd told Stone, Ajay, a whole room full of trolls and mermaids and, of course, Lord Volderiss and Nate. I'd done a tap dance on the radar. Now I'd tangled with Gilligan and Sky, and I was dating the Prime Elite, king of all the Creatures. Yeah, okay, I was breakdancing on the radar.

'Not so much,' I muttered.

Audrey looked amused. 'No,' she agreed, 'not so much.'

Cuth continued. 'They knew they'd die a week after your eighteenth birthday. Soon after your birth, they summoned us – they asked their nearest and dearest friends to help them. By that point The Twenty, Faltease's Fallen, were dropping like flies. The fear in the community was palpable. They asked for our help and of course we gave it to them. We performed a rite – the wizard, the seer, the witch, the dragon and the griffin. And I made the tea,' he added mildly.

I wanted to smile at that, but I was so tense, and I needed to know so much that I just wanted him to get to the damned point. Emory let out a low growl, and I knew he felt the same.

'The rite was twofold. First the circle bound your parents' magic so they couldn't be tracked or scried by a witch. Then they prepared a consciousness transference rite, but didn't complete it.'

I was grateful I was sitting down. I was gripping the sofa's edge so tightly that my knuckles were white. I wished Emory was next to me. As if the thought had summoned him, he crossed to my sofa and slipped his arm around my shoulders, bracing me for what was to come.

'They prepared to transfer their consciousness?' I asked, my throat tight. 'To what?' I thought of Glimmer, the dagger that seemed more conscious than inanimate, and I felt a chill of dread.

'To *whom*,' Cuthbert corrected softly. 'The griffin in our enterprise could also coax. To do that, he had to be able to communicate in a way that transcended mere language. He could coax someone whose language he couldn't speak because he could understand their thoughts, no matter the means of communication.'

I reached up and gripped Emory's hand. 'Who?' I demanded.

'This is supposition on my part, but your parents knew that they died a week after your eighteenth birthday. They summoned Bastion and hired him to kill their bodies *after* they had completed the rite we had started so long ago.'

'Who?' I growled.

Cuthbert met my fiery gaze with soft sympathetic

eyes. 'Someone they had loved and trusted since their earliest days in the Other realm. Their constant, their companion.'

It clicked then. All I felt was a roaring white noise in my ears which all but drowned out Cuthbert's next word. 'Gato.'

CHAPTER 16

I BLINKED. EMORY was hugging me, rocking me back and forth soothingly like I was a child. My breathing was fast and shallow, and my ears were ringing. I felt dizzy, sick. 'Can I have a drink?' I said, my voice echoey and distant to my own ears. I was thirsty, incredibly thirsty.

'She's going into shock,' Audrey said, her voice laced with concern.

No shit, Sherlock.

Emory wrapped a blanket around my shoulders. It should have felt stifling in the roasting-hot house, but my skin was cold and clammy and I was grateful for something to hug around me.

Emory carefully pushed me backwards. 'Lie down, Jess,' he ordered.

I complied, letting him manoeuvre me into lying flat on the sofa. My mind was wonderfully, deliciously blank. I knew there was something itching to be dealt with but just now my mind was taking a holiday.

My mobile phone rang, repeatedly, insistently. Finally

Emory relented and answered for me. 'Nate, it's Emory. Jinx has had some news. She's in shock… She'll be fine… No, you don't need to come. Just – can you and Hes and Gato get to her house and stay there? We'll be back as soon as we can.'

He rang off. Hearing Gato's name tugged at my mind. There was something I should be dealing with, but I boxed it off. I lay on Audrey's comfortable sofa with a blanket around my shoulders and my mind.

'I'm getting her a potion,' Emory said finally.

Audrey disagreed. 'She needs to work her way through this. Potions aren't always the right answer. She's had a shock and her body is processing it. Soon her mind will, too. Leave her, let her rest.'

Emory swore loudly and impressively. Who knew the king had such a potty mouth? He lifted me into his arms and carried me effortlessly into Audrey and Cuthbert's spare room, undressed me quickly and efficiently and tucked me into bed. He paced at the foot of the bed, worry cascading down our bond.

'Stay,' I said softly.

His shoulders slumped and the tension flew out of him. He nodded and climbed on the bed next to me. Then he pulled me close, and my fuzzy head tumbled into sleep.

I AWOKE WRAPPED in Emory's embrace. The sun was streaming in because he hadn't drawn the curtains. I paused in my automatic examination of the room. I knew this room, I'd been here before. It was Audrey and Cuthbert's house. Like a key in the lock, something clicked in my mind and everything rushed back to me.

My parents were alive, locked in my hell hound. They had never died. All those years of grief, and they'd been alive the whole time. I had a moment of bizarre muddle-headed relief that I'd only acquired Gato after my grief-induced tailspin into sex, drugs and rock and roll had ended. By the time Leo Harfen had given Gato to me, I'd already started my private investigator business. Gato had ridden shotgun from the start; he'd always had my back, he'd always been so damned smart.

People had commented that he was clever, even for a hell hound, and still I hadn't thought of him as anything out of the ordinary. I mean, he was a hell hound, so of course he was out of the ordinary. But I thought then of the thousand cuddles he'd given me, licks and kisses – moments where I could have sworn he winked at me. It had been my parents, staring at me through my dog's eyes.

I'd dropped my empathy shield a time or two around Gato, and I'd felt such a pervading sense of love. I'd put it down to a dog's loyalty but it wasn't that, wasn't the love of a pet, but the all-consuming love of parents who would do anything to keep me safe. Including, it transpired, faking their own deaths, destroying their bodies and transferring their consciousness to their dog so they could still be part of my life.

When I'd had my jaunt back in time, I'd told my parents that they had died. I had told them when, and from that moment I'd fixed their deaths as a certainty. All they had to do was work it so that their deaths never took place even though they appeared to.

Mrs H had reported their deaths to the Connection, and the hunter of Faltease's Twenty had drawn a line through their names. But Mrs H was the seer who'd helped them; she'd known who she was dog-sitting all of those times I'd left Gato with her. I felt guilt rise anew at her death. She'd been a good friend to my parents, had helped to raise me, and I'd killed her. Still, she had been trying to take over the Connection and raise her daughter from the dead to start a sinister dynasty, so…

Emory woke. He lay still as he searched my eyes. 'You're back,' he said with palpable relief.

'Yes, sorry about that. I guess I checked out for a little while.' Again. Sheesh, I was a liability.

'Understandable. How do you feel?'

I threw him a shaky smile. 'That's a complicated question. They did all of this to protect me but, damn it, it hurt so much. Couldn't they have let me in on the charade? I can keep a secret – they knew that. I never told a soul I was a truth seeker, but they still kept it from me that they were alive.' I bit my lip. 'I'm happy and angry. I'm relieved and dismayed. So many tears, so much grief and loss, it informed who I am. It changed everything and it changed me. And none of it was real. Who am I now?'

Emory pulled me close. 'You're Jinx, Jessica Sharp. You're my mate, the love of my life, best friend to Lucy. Your foundations might have been shaken, but you're still you.'

'Lucy,' I whispered, swallowing hard. I rolled out of Emory's arms and reached for my phone on the bedside table. I dialled her number without conscious effort.

She answered straight away. 'Ugh. Jess, somebody had better be dead. We were out until 5 a.m. and we're still tired.' I could picture her, eyes muzzy with sleep, blonde hair ruffled and still looking perfect.

'I need you,' I managed.

'Jess? What's up?' Her voice was sharper, alert.

'I need you,' I repeated. 'Can you come? To my house?'

'I'm packing a bag. I'll be four hours tops.'

I fought against the welling of tears in my eyes. Lucy always had my back. 'I love you.'

'I love you too, Jess. I'm on my way. Hold on.'

Though she couldn't see me, I nodded and then hung up. She didn't ask for any explanation other than that she was needed, and she was on her way. True friendship like that is worth everything.

Emory was watching me. 'Lucy is a piper now. She can talk to Gato, to your parents.'

'I hope so.' I hoped so, and at the same time I dreaded it. What would they say? What could *I* say? I couldn't even begin to imagine the conversation.

I gave Emory a reassuring kiss and slid out of the bed to the bathroom. A shower would help to clear my head.

By the end of thirty minutes under the pouring hot water, my mind was still somewhat numb. The idea that my parents were alive in some form or another was going to take some getting used to.

Emory had gone from the room when I emerged, prune-like, from the shower. Audrey had lain out some fresh clothes for me to pull on: a long black skirt and a simple white blouse. Not my usual fare but I'd take it. I was happy not to be pulling on clothes I'd already worn.

I went in search of food. All conversation stopped as I walked into the dining room. I took the chair next to Emory, grabbed a slice of toast and buttered it in total silence. Finally I looked up. 'I'm not going to break,' I said in exasperation. 'It was a shock, it still is a shock, but I'm a girl who can roll with the punches. You don't need to tiptoe on eggshells around me.'

'I'm glad to see you're feeling more yourself, my dear.' Audrey offered me some jam.

I took it; it was a jam morning if ever there was one. 'Thanks.'

Cuthbert cleared his throat and continued the conversation I'd interrupted. 'It's all over the news. First Cumberland Street and now this. They're blaming it on sinkholes.'

'How certain are we that it was the ouroboros again?' Emory asked.

Cuthbert snorted. 'Certain. There were so many eye witnesses. Someone isn't trying to be subtle. This last attack was sizeable – three homes fell into the hole. If the Connection hadn't been there, many would have died. As it was, a child had a broken arm. Inspector Stone and our Ajay had to wipe all of the Commoners of the memory of the ouroboros. The Other's magic started to break down in the face of a giant worm, and some of the Commoners saw it. Ajay says that so many people had to be cleared that they had to call in back-up.'

He shook his head. 'This is a serious threat to the Verdict. There are only so many sinkholes the Common realm will accept before they realise something fishy is going on. Someone needs to bring that worm down.'

Emory sighed. 'Why do I feel like that comment was aimed at me?'

'Because it was,' Cuthbert said flatly. 'You're the Prime *Elite*. You rule the creatures.'

'Not that one,' Emory protested. His skin warmed

slightly. 'I did try ordering it but it didn't work.'

'I'm not saying you have to reason with it, I'm saying you have to deal with it. This is your responsibility now, my boy,' Cuthbert said forcefully. 'When you tacked on that "Elite" to your title, it meant more than just letting the mermaids flash their tails at you.'

'Are you getting told off?' I said gleefully.

'Scolded,' Emory agreed glumly. 'I feel like I'm fourteen again.'

'Like the time we caught you with a picture showing a lady's elbow,' Audrey chimed in.

'Elbow?' I asked, amused.

'The Victorians were weird about showing elbows,' Emory said defensively.

'And did this lady have very shapely elbows?' I enquired solicitously.

'Yours are nicer,' he promised.

Despite myself, I reddened. Jeez, even a compliment about my elbows made me blush. I'm a ridiculous human.

'So our plan for the day is to deal with a giant worm?' I asked, once I'd finished eating.

'No,' Emory said firmly. 'The plan is to go to your house, find Lucy and talk to your parents.'

'The ouroboros—'

'Can wait. We don't know where it is, or where it will pop up next. At this point, we have no option but to firefight. I'll get Tom and his team on it, but right now our priority is you. And if we can talk to your parents, maybe we can glean more about who was killing The Twenty.'

'You're bossy,' I pointed out.

His lips curved up in a smile. 'You love it.'

I didn't argue because he wasn't wrong.

CHAPTER 17

THE DRIVE HOME only took an hour but it was the longest hour of my life. I stopped the car a hundred yards from my house and turned to Emory. 'I can't do this,' I said honestly. 'What if this is all a huge hoax and my parents are still dead?'

'If it's a hoax, I'll throttle Cuthbert,' Emory promised. 'But it's not. This is real, Jess.'

I shook my head. 'It's too hard. I can't let myself hope. If it's not true – to have them given back and then snatched away—' I couldn't even articulate my feelings.

Emory took my hand. 'I'm here. I'll support you however I can.'

I raised his hand to my mouth and kissed the back of it. 'I know you will. I know Lucy will. Gato—' I blew out a sigh. 'Gato always supports me too.'

'He won't stop now,' Emory said gently.

I nodded and released Emory's hand. Time to pull on my big-girl pants. I started the car again and drove the short distance onto my drive. I got out of the car, beeping it locked behind us. As I unlocked the front door, there was a welcoming bark and Gato gambolled downstairs, wagging enthusiastically. He'd missed me. And he – *they* – didn't know that anything had changed.

Everything had changed.

Nate and Hes were in the living room, and they called out to us. 'What happened?' Nate demanded, sounding concerned. 'You were so upset.' He crossed the distance between us and pulled me into his arms. His friendship settled over me.

I nodded against his shoulder. 'Yeah, I was.' I gave him a squeeze before stepping back. 'But before I discuss it with you two, I need some alone time with Gato. Gato?' I called for him to follow me up to my bedroom. Emory touched my arm as I passed him, but he settled downstairs with Nate and Hes to give me some privacy.

Gato followed me up the stairs but the jubilant bounce was gone from his step. He knew something was up. I went into my bedroom and tapped the bed. He jumped up next to me, turning three times before he settled. It made me smile just the tiniest bit. I sat on the bed next to him and he laid his great head in my lap and waited expectantly.

'It's been a crazy few days,' I started. 'I should have realised when we met with Jake Winters that more was going on than I realised. He asked you if you'd done it, and you said yes. I spoke to Bastion, to Audrey and Cuthbert. Cuthbert wasn't bound by your geas. Did you know?'

Gato was unnaturally still, hardly even breathing. He looked at me unblinkingly.

I continued. 'He told me you transferred your consciousness into Gato. That you're both living in my dog. Is it true? Or am I finally losing it?'

Gato looked at me for one long moment before he gave a definite nod. This was insane; this was crazy. Absurd, ridiculous. My eyes filled with tears. 'Really?' I whispered. 'You promise you're both really in there?'

Gato nodded again. He sat up and hooked his head around me in his equivalent of a hug. I lost my shit and started to bawl in open-mouthed sobs that were neither delicate nor pretty. Through it all, Gato whined softly and hugged me. When the tears dried, he – *they* – licked my face and made me smile.

'Yeah,' I muttered, 'turn that frown upside down. I hear you, Ma.' I took several steadying breaths. 'I'm so happy, so relieved. So damn confused. And a tiny bit angry. Okay, a lot angry,' I admitted.

Gato bowed his head and let out a soft whine. 'You took yourselves away from me. I thought you were *dead*. For years. I—' I shook my head as tears threatened again. Yeah, the anger was there alright. This conversation was too hard to do one-sided.

I checked the time. 'Lucy will be here soon. I don't know how good her piping skills are, but hopefully she'll be able to communicate with you. If not, I can call

Bastion. I wish you'd told me you were friends with him. You know, you could have purred at him or something.'

Gato's ears flattened. 'So you're not a cat, but you know what I mean. Let's go on down. Nate will be bursting with curiosity. And I – I can't quite cope with this. I'm happy you're both alive, I want you to know that. But I'm mixed up, I don't know where my head is. Just give me some time to let this sink in.'

Gato nodded, his eyes sad. I couldn't leave it like that. I gave him one last cuddle. 'I love you so much. This is a miracle,' I whispered, before whirling around and rushing down to join the others. Gato followed me ponderously downstairs.

Emory stood up as I walked in, eyebrows raised in question. I nodded, flung myself into his arms and he held me firmly against him. 'I'm so pleased for you, Jess.'

He pressed a kiss to my forehead and suddenly I felt a little guilty. He'd lost his family so long ago, and by all accounts his father had been a drunk and a wastrel. I was getting a second chance, but there wasn't one for him. He met my eyes. 'I'm happy for you,' he repeated, kissing me again.

He released me from his arms and faced Gato. 'My honour to meet you,' Emory greeted my parents, touching his hand to his heart and bowing low. Gato bounded forwards and gave him a giant lick that made him grin. 'I think they approve of me.'

I rolled my eyes. 'Of course they approve of you. You're handsome and kind, and you shower me with ridiculous gifts and food. What more could they want for me?'

'Happiness?'

'I am happy – happier than I ever thought I'd be.'

'Okay,' Hes interrupted. 'I'm trying hard to be patient but this is actually killing me. What gives? What's the big bad secret you're all talking about in code?'

I trusted Hes and Nate completely, so I told them. 'My parents did a consciousness transference rite. Their bodies are dead, but their souls – their minds – are in Gato.'

Hes's mouth dropped open.

'Close your mouth or you'll catch flies,' I parroted one of my mother's favourite sayings.

Her jaw clacked shut and she blinked several times. 'That's amazing! Weird! But so cool!'

'Weird but so cool should be the tagline for my whole life,' I griped.

'I've heard of spells like that,' Nate said slowly, 'but I've never heard of them being successful before. They require a great sacrifice, like any dicey magic.'

'Like their bodies being killed?' I suggested.

Nate grimaced. 'Sure, that might do it.'

Hes looked at Gato. 'Nice to meet you, Mr and Mrs Sharp,' she said to him, then muttered, 'Man that feels weird.' Gato barked and wagged his tail at her.

There was a knock at the door – Lucy! I sprang to open it but it wasn't my friend. It was Amber DeLea, and she looked crushed in a way I hadn't seen before. Her eyes were oddly vacant. 'Amber?' I asked.

She met my eyes with her dull, lifeless ones. 'Jake's dead,' she said.

CHAPTER 18

I USHERED AMBER into my lounge and sat her down. The modest room was looking a little cramped, but Gato helped by lying down on the floor out of the way. 'What happened?' I asked softly.

Amber shook her head. 'I don't believe it,' she said, her voice showing some signs of life. 'I don't care what it looks like.'

'What does it look like?' I queried gently.

'Like he killed himself,' she replied bluntly. 'Jake struggled sometimes, and he had terrible lows, but he was so happy after your visit. He was buoyed up. I just can't see him hurting himself now, after all this time. It doesn't make sense.' Her eyes filled with tears. 'He was *hopeful*.'

My emotions were close to the surface, and it killed me as I saw Gato curl into a tight ball, his head wrapped around his body tightly as if my parents were giving themselves a hug.

My gut was talking to me loudly. I didn't believe Jake had killed himself, either. God, I didn't want to be right about this.

I pulled my phone out and dialled Bastion. He answered, as usual, with silence. 'Were you hired to kill Jake Winters?' I asked abruptly, dreading the answer.

On the sofa, Amber froze.

There was a long silence. 'You know I can't answer that,' Bastion said finally.

'You could, if you hadn't done it,' I hung up. I was struggling to sort out my feelings for Bastion. He cared for me deeply and he'd protected me, but he killed people for a living. How did I reconcile that?

I met Amber's eyes. 'I'm sorry. Bastion can coax. If Jake had even a hint of a suicidal idea…'

Anger and relief warred in her eyes. 'Jake didn't kill himself. He was killed.'

I nodded. 'He didn't choose to leave you. He hadn't given up.'

Amber broke down. I wrapped my arms around her as she sobbed, and I lowered my mental shields to feel her. Grief, thick and rolling, came off her in waves.

Amber knew where Jake lived, and she'd protected him for years, so I thought there was little to no chance she was involved in his death – but I had to be sure. As I searched her emotions, there was nothing in her but loss. No guilt, no duplicitousness. I let the ocean roar back into place and comforted her while she cried.

Hes and Nate had departed discreetly, leaving Emory, Gato and I with the grieving witch. If Amber wasn't involved in Jake's death then I had the sinking feeling that I was. In all the years Amber had hidden him, she had never taken guests to visit him. Then she took me and a few days later he was dead. Someone was tracking my movements – and the only ones I knew who were doing that were Emory and his team. I had the sinking feeling that we had a mole and I'd led them right to Jake. Guilt burned inside me, hot and uncomfortable.

Emory touched my arm. He could feel the guilt down our bond. *We led them to Jake,* I mouthed. *We have a mole.*

He blinked as he tried to read my lips before a dark frown descended. His jaw clenched. He dug out his phone and left the room. Someone that we trusted wasn't to be trusted.

Eventually Amber's tears dried up. I went to the kitchen to make her a coffee and found Emory propped against the kitchen counter. 'Hey.' He greeted me with a kiss. 'As far as I can see, the only ones who had access to your location were Manners, Tom, Ajay, Summer, Hes and my tech guy, Fritz.'

I didn't like that Hes was on the list, and I *really* didn't like that the list was so small. Of the names listed, Fritz and Summer were the only unknowns. 'I'll have to speak to them,' I said reluctantly.

Emory rubbed a hand over his face. He didn't like it any more than I did. 'Yeah,' he agreed. 'I'll arrange it. I don't want them at your house until we know who the threat is.'

'Are you going to pull Manners and Tom off security detail?'

'I'm not taking any chances with you. If someone did give that information out, they can't be trusted. They might even be linked to the attempts to kill you.'

'The attempts to kill me don't feel very serious,' I argued. 'Come on, death by spider?'

Emory frowned. '*You* need to take this seriously.'

'I am, trust me. But something just doesn't fit. I think someone's trying to distract us again.'

'From what?'

I sighed. 'That's the million-pound question, isn't it? It could be the ouroboros, it could be the deaths of Faltease's Fallen. It could be someone trying to distract you from politics. If it's that, maybe you should touch base with Roscoe.'

'Ajay keeps me informed of the symposium's meetings.'

'Ajay's on the list,' I pointed out gently. 'Roscoe isn't. And Ajay isn't a political creature. At the end of the day he's a cop, and he might miss some nuances. Roscoe is in the room. Speak to him, see if anything else gets flagged. And let's see what we can do about that damned worm.'

'We can put a tracking device on it next time it rears up,' Emory suggested.

'You'll need to get the tracking device from someone other than Fritz,' I pointed out.

'This sucks. I trust my team.'

'I know you do, just as I trust Hes. But for now, everyone except us is a suspect.'

'Hes might have told Nate,' Emory said reluctantly. His bias was showing; he wanted a vampyr to be the leak.

I opened my mouth to protest and closed it again. 'I'm sure Hes swore she wouldn't tell anyone about our visit to Jake, and she was telling the truth at the time. But I'll follow it up. No stone unturned,' I promised.

Emory looked grim, and I didn't blame him. Our core team had become our core suspects, and it wasn't a comfortable feeling for either of us.

'Call in Tom,' I suggested. 'I can use my truth seeking on him and we can find out if we can trust him. We'll do the same with Manners and that will be two suspects down.'

Emory went to get Tom, and I sent Hes a quick text: *Where did you go? You okay?*

Almost immediately I received a response: *I've got classes soon, and then I'll stay tonight at Nate's. xx*

OK. Stay safe. x

You too. xx

I bit my lip. For now, Hes had to remain on the suspect list. My gut didn't like it at all, but I'd been tricked before by some clever wordsmithing. Fool me once, shame on you; fool me twice, fuck you. So yeah, she was still on the list.

I took Amber her coffee. 'Sorry it took me a minute,' I hesitated. How much to say? 'I think someone must have tracked us to Jake's house. Someone has been trying to kill me – you know, with the runes and all? Someone might be watching me. I'm sorry.'

Amber's eyes were cool and hard. Her face bore the ravages of tears but her voice was steady and even. 'Yes,' she agreed, 'it seems too coincidental that you visited and then he was killed. I'm not accusing you, or saying you're personally involved, but someone was tracking you.'

I nodded but didn't tell her that Emory was tracking me. 'Someone's determined to finish off killing Faltease's Fallen.'

She sipped her coffee. 'We're going to finish them instead.' *True.*

'Yes, we are. I'm done with running from this.'

'Good. I'm in – all in – until this is done.'

'The more the merrier.' I cleared my throat. 'I found out about my parents, transferring into Gato.'

Her eyebrows shot up. 'Did you now? And how did you break my geas?'

'I didn't. I found someone who hadn't been bound by it who knew what was going on. I've summoned a friend – a piper, someone I trust – to speak to my parents and find out what they know.'

Amber pursed her lips. 'Good. Your mum was a truth seeker. If anyone knows more about what's going on, it is her.'

'So Jake told me,' I admitted.

Amber's eyes filled. 'Fuck.' She dashed angrily at her tears. I didn't offer false comfort. What more was there to say? She'd lost the man she loved, and even worse, she'd barely managed to have him at all.

Emory knocked on the door jamb. 'Sorry to intrude. I've got Tom here. Manners is watching the outside.'

'Bring him in here,' I suggested.

Emory dipped his head towards Amber in question.

'She deserves to know,' I said bitterly. I wasn't a fan of keeping people in the dark, not when it affected them. I'd been in the dark myself way too many times lately, and It wasn't a good place to be.

Emory let Tom in and gestured at him to sit down. Tom was a hulking great muscley man, and he made my armchair look small. He didn't seem nervous; if anything, he was curious.

'I'm a truth seeker,' I said.

Amber didn't react at all. Tom's eyes widened – but was that in alarm or surprise?

I concentrated and let the ocean recede, separating the emotions tangling around me: Amber's grief, Emory's worry, Tom's curiosity and surprise. But there was no sense of alarm, no panic.

'I need to ask you some questions,' I said to Tom. 'I'm sorry about this, but we need to be sure.' After reading him, I already felt pretty sure but 'pretty sure' wasn't good enough. 'Are you loyal to Emory?'

'Yes.' Tom responded without hesitation. *True.*

'Have you passed on sensitive knowledge to any third parties?'

'No.' *True.*

'Did you tell anyone where Jake Winters lived?'

'No.' *True.*

'Have you told anyone about my whereabouts?'

'I've told Emory and Manners your location when they've asked about it.' *True.*

I turned to the others. 'He's telling the truth. I'm confident he's not our leak. Does anyone else have questions we need to ask?'

Amber and Emory shook their heads. I didn't want to question Tom more than necessary. He was on our team, but an intense interrogation would erode anyone's loyalty.

'I'm sorry for questioning you,' I said to him.

Tom waved it away. 'We have a leak?'

Emory nodded. 'We were monitoring Jinx's location and someone passed on the location of Jake's house. Now Jake is dead. We suspect he was killed by Bastion, but that hasn't been confirmed.'

Tom's jaw tightened. 'We should ask Bastion who hired him.'

'He won't tell us,' Emory explained.

'You're the Prime Elite,' Tom growled. 'We'll *make* him tell us, if necessary.'

I interrupted, 'If we can get to Bastion, I can divine who hired him, but first we need him to come to me. He knows what I can do, so I doubt he'll come willingly. For now, let's rule out Manners.'

Tom rose. 'I'll get him.'

He escorted Manners in a few moments later. Manners' blond hair was still a shocking pink but somehow it suited him; annoyingly, with his tan skin and muscled physique, he managed to pull it off. He looked around the room with his usual jaunty arrogance. 'What gives?' he asked lightly. He was curious; there was no hint of guile or panic.

I decided to get straight to it. 'Did you tell anyone where Jake Winters lived?'

'No. Why would I?' *True.*

I ignored his question. 'Are you loyal to Emory?'

'Yes,' Manners responded fiercely. *True.*

'Have you passed on sensitive knowledge to any third parties?'

He raised his eyebrows but answered the question anyway. 'Never.' *True.*

'Have you told anyone about my whereabouts?'

'I've told our team your location when asked.'

'Who is your team?'

'The Prime, Tom, Ajay, Fritz and Summer.' *True.*

'Alright. All done. He's telling the truth.'

'You're a truth seeker,' Manners growled. 'That's why you believed Stone could be trusted to storm the castle with us.'

'Bingo.'

'I want all of you to swear an oath that you won't knowingly reveal Jinx's truth-seeking skills to anyone else.' Emory included Amber as he glared around the room. He got nods all round. 'Verbally, so it's binding and Jinx knows you're telling the truth.'

They all muttered their oaths; each one *was* telling the truth.

'Now Tom and I are in the clear, who else is on the shit list?' Manners asked.

'Summer, Fritz and Ajay,' Emory confirmed.

'And Hes,' I interjected.

Tom shook his head. 'That little girl wouldn't betray you. She thinks the sun rises in your eyes. You're her hero.'

I shifted uncomfortably; I wanted a friend, not a follower. 'I don't think the leak came from her. She promised she wouldn't tell anyone and she was telling the truth. Unless something major changed, I can't see her breaking her word. But she's on the list. Everyone's on the list until they're eliminated.'

It was interesting – and alarming – that neither Tom nor Manners rushed in to affirm Summer, Fritz or Ajay's loyalty. That was something to worry about.

CHAPTER 19

A LOUD KNOCK at the door interrupted the moment. I went to open it and gave a loud squeal of delight. I all but leapt into my best friend's arms. 'Lucy!'

She dropped her duffle bag and threw her arms around me. 'I'm here. Where's the fire?'

'Fucking everywhere,' I muttered into her shoulder. 'Help.'

She drew back in surprise. 'I can count on one hand the number of times you've asked for help.'

'Apparently I'm stubborn.'

She grinned at me. 'Wouldn't have you any other way.'

'Come in. I've got a lot to tell you,' I said.

She picked up her duffle and followed me in. It wasn't fair; she'd been jerked out of bed early, come in a hurry, and she still looked pristine. No make-up, sure, but her golden hair was as perfect as always, her jeans were clean and her cute blouse looked ironed.

I could always count on Lucy. The world could implode but she'd always turn up when I called, and she'd always look a million dollars. Something in me eased. The world was topsy-turvy, but she was here.

I popped my head into the lounge. 'Lucy's here. I'm just going to take her upstairs and fill her in on a few things.'

'Can she be trusted?' Manners asked levelly.

I glared. 'Of course she can!'

'You said everyone's on the list.'

'Everyone who knew Jake's location. She didn't know it, so she's not on the list. She's as far away from the list as you can get.'

'I don't mind being tested,' Lucy interjected. 'I'd rather you know for sure that I can be trusted one hundred percent.'

'I *do* know that.' I glared at Manners some more.

'I don't,' Manners argued. 'If you're bringing her into the circle of trust, test her.'

'Fine,' I conceded angrily. 'But I don't like you right now.'

'I don't rightly care,' he retorted. *Lie.*

That broke through to me. He was only protecting Emory and, by extension, me. I deflated. 'Sorry,' I muttered. 'I'll test her, then I'll tell her. Come on, Luce, let's go upstairs.'

Gato rose and then hesitated. I rolled my eyes. 'Yeah, you lot may as well come too.' He wagged and thundered up to my bedroom. Lucy and I followed at a more sedate pace then settled on my bed to talk.

'I'm sorry to ask all these questions,' I started awkwardly.

'Just shoot, Jess, then we can get onto the meaty stuff.'

'Sure. Did you know or tell anyone where Jake Winters lived?'

'No.' *True.*

'Are you loyal to me?'

'Yes,' Lucy responded firmly. *True.*

'Have you passed on sensitive knowledge to any third parties?'

'No.' *True.*

'Have you told anyone about my whereabouts?'

'No. I told Lord Samuel I was coming to meet you, but I didn't say where. We shared a ride up here, but I dropped him off in Liverpool. He said he had pack business.' *True.*

'You passed. Now, let's get on to the nitty-gritty.' I told her in greater detail about the attempts on my life and my belief that there was more to them than met the eye. I told her about the ouroboros, and finally I told her about Jake and Faltease's Fallen.

'Are you done?' she asked when I finally paused for breath.

I shook my head. 'No, the worst is yet to come,' I admitted.

I told her about Amber and Sky, about meeting with

Audrey and Cuthbert. Finally we reached the crunch point. 'Cuth told me that my parents used a rite to transfer their consciousness from their bodies to their dog.'

Lucy's mouth dropped open, and she turned to Gato, slack jawed. 'Your parents are in Gato?'

'My parents *are* Gato. They've been there the whole time I've had him. Every wag, every cuddle, every lick…' I trailed off. 'It was them the whole time.'

All credit to Lucy that she didn't freak out. She blinked rapidly, trying to process it. 'Mr Sharp, Mrs Sharp,' she greeted them finally. 'It's so wonderful you're alive, albeit trapped in a dog.' Gato barked. 'Excuse me, hell hound,' she corrected herself politely.

'I was hoping you could help,' I said softly. 'You're a piper, right? Can you talk to them?'

Lucy deflated and folded in on herself. 'We've been wondering about that, Esme and I. Esme and I can talk – we have a connection unlike any other werewolf we've heard about – but we haven't managed to communicate with any other animals. Not ants, not rabbits, not deer. I'm sorry. Maybe you're wrong about me being a piper.'

'I'm sure the last person I stabbed before you was a piper,' I muttered, casting my mind back. Ronan was definitely the one I'd stabbed before Lucy.

'It's worrying that you have to think that long about it,' Lucy remarked.

'Things have been dicey.'

'No kidding.'

I bit my lip. 'I was kind of counting on you being able to speak to Gato. I can't let any Tom, Dick or Harry know about them. I can't trust them to another piper.'

'Maybe Emory knows someone who can show me the ropes,' Lucy suggested. 'Maybe I just need a pointer in the right direction.'

'Maybe.'

We went downstairs to re-join the others. 'Any luck?' Emory asked, looking at Gato.

Lucy shook her head. 'I'm sorry. I don't know how to pipe yet.'

Manners raised an eyebrow. 'You're a piper who doesn't know how to pipe?'

'I'm a werewolf who may have some piping skills, but they've never been verified,' Lucy retorted, giving as good as she got. Manners held his hands up in a placatory gesture.

'Do you know a piper we can trust?' I asked Emory.

He frowned. 'I know someone, but the last time we saw each other we weren't on good terms. I'll put a feeler out.'

'Lisette?' Tom asked.

Emory nodded.

'Dylan speaks well of her,' Manners commented.

'Yeah, I'll get Dylan to reach out.' Emory clicked away

at his phone before a whoosh signalled that an email had been sent. 'I've arranged for you to meet with Summer shortly,' he said to me. 'We're still trying to nail down Fritz and Ajay. I called Roscoe and you were right, he had some interesting news. The trolls and ogres have both sided with the anti-creature movement on the last couple of votes, and it's tipped the balance of power in their favour. By all accounts, Stone is leading the charge. He's been pointing out the destruction the ouroboros has left in its wake as a reason to curtail creature freedom – for the good of all, of course.'

'What do you mean, curtailing your freedom?' I asked.

'He wants the creatures tagged so their movements can be tracked. He's selling the idea that it will make it easier to track down the next rogue creature.'

I stared. 'Tagged? Like criminals? That's ridiculous. It's barbaric.'

'His anti-creature sentiments were well-masked, or maybe it wasn't so strong before. With the death of his father at the hands of a griffin, the gloves are now off.' Emory's tone was bitter.

'He doesn't *know* that Bastion killed Lord Gilligan,' I protested.

'We do, so why couldn't he?'

That stumped me. 'You can't tag entire species like cattle because of one bad egg,' I said stubbornly.

'We're on the same page, Jess. I'm just repeating what Roscoe said. Roscoe did well in solidifying his power base after we spoke a few days ago, but he's still not strong enough to rock the boat. He's keeping out of it as much as he can, but he said there's a big vote coming up soon about the curtailing measures.'

'About tagging you like animals.' Emory nodded. 'You wouldn't agree to it,' I said flatly.

'No,' he replied mildly.

'What would that mean?' I asked.

'It would mean the end of any semblance of co-operation with the Connection. It would mean war.'

CHAPTER 20

E MORY'S PHONE BEEPED. 'Dylan says he can take us to Lisette, but it has to be now because he has herd business later. I'll push back the meeting with Summer.' He turned to Tom. 'Put her on ice for now.'

Tom nodded and spoke to Manners. 'You drive them to Lisette.'

Amber stood up. 'I'm coming too. I'm seeing this through.'

I nodded my agreement and we all piled into my Mercedes, Manners and Emory at the front, Amber, Lucy and I in the back, and Gato in the boot. 'This is a circus,' I murmured.

'A powerful one,' Amber snorted. 'The King of the dragons, a werewolf, a witch and an empath.'

Manners stiffened in the front. 'You just keep on looking pretty in pink, darling,' Amber taunted him.

His shoulders relaxed. 'I do look good,' he shot back, focusing on the road.

We drove for half an hour out into rural Cheshire and parked near a farm. What I thought was a horse started to move towards us. It wasn't a horse; it was a centaur.

'He's not wearing trousers,' I commented to Lucy. 'Where am I supposed to look?'

'At his face,' Emory advised, amused.

'But his … it's just dangling there,' I said in a strangled voice. 'Shouldn't he put trousers on?'

'And how is he supposed to put them on?' Emory asked. 'Is he supposed to sit while he wrestles them on one leg at a time?'

'All the centaurs could help each other get dressed,' I suggested. 'Like a big co-operative.'

'He's coming over,' Emory pointed out. 'Can you chill?'

'Oh, I'm ice, baby,' I promised. I was not ice; I was awkward and infantile. And the centaur's wang was right there. I mean he was hung … like an actual horse, and it was just out there, loud and proud and huge. I looked fixedly at his brown eyes, but I could still see the angle of his dangle in my peripheral vision.

His long brunette hair swept down his neck, curling at his shoulders. He looked like every centaur ever depicted, complete with hooves and tail. And wang. There was no way you could forget the wang.

'If I wasn't very secure in our relationship and my sexuality,' Emory murmured to me, 'I'd be feeling insecure about this whole thing.'

'I don't think you've been insecure about anything your whole life,' I retorted.

'You'd be surprised.' Emory stepped forwards. 'Dylan, thank you for meeting with me at such short notice.'

'It is my honour to serve you, Prime Elite. The herd is strongest together.'

'The herd is strongest together. Tell me, you've said you trust Lisette. She's never given you reason to doubt her?'

'Since you delivered her to us, she has been most helpful,' Dylan said firmly.

Emory winced a little at Dylan's phraseology. 'I'm glad she has assisted you. Has she ... warmed to her post?'

'I believe she is less irate. It's sometimes hard to tell. Gin helps. She is looking forward to seeing you. But she hasn't had any gin yet,' he warned.

Emory chewed his bottom lip. 'Lead on then.' He looked back at me, his dark-green eyes unreadable, then he started forwards.

My gut curled uncomfortably. I wasn't going to like this.

Dylan led us to a paddock where there were about thirteen goats. There was also a brunette whose hair was dusted with silver. I'd guess her age at around the mid-fifties but time had been kind to her. Her face had soft lines of age, but she was still a remarkable beauty. Her expression was unreadable.

She stood as she heard the gate creak open. 'Tom. Emory.' Her tone wasn't friendly. 'You can take yourselves right back off my land.'

'Lisette,' Emory greeted her, ignoring her instructions. 'You're looking well.'

'Old. I'm looking old. And you look not a day older than the day you abandoned me here to rot.'

'I didn't abandon you,' he objected. 'I bought you this land and you said you'd be happy here.'

'I said *we'd* be happy here,' she countered bitterly.

Of course – she was an ex of Emory's. I guessed that after a couple of centuries he had to have a few. It seemed that, although their affair had ended some time ago, Lisette still held a grudge. I couldn't blame her. I'd be bitter, too, if Emory left me.

'I told you, we aren't mates. We never could be,' Emory said, his voice still calm.

'And she is?' she asked stridently, pointing at me. 'That slip of a girl is your choice?' Her voice was full of scorn.

That was enough to chivvy me forwards; I wasn't going to be a passive member of this conversation. 'I'm Jinx and this is Lucy. Lucy has recently learned about the Other realm. She's supposed to be a piper, but she doesn't know the first thing about it.'

'And you're here for pointers? From me?' Lisette sneered.

'Yes, if you can remove your head from your ass long enough to give them,' I retorted, hands on hips.

She sent me a condescending smirk. 'The kitten meows. How cute.'

The Other realm was all about showing strength. No one needed to know that it was pure bravado. I smiled back nicely. 'This kitten has ripped her enemies into little pieces, and I'm not averse to doing the same to you, little mouse, if you won't help my friend.' *Lie.*

Lisette barked a laugh. 'Well then, come here, Lucy. Let's see what can be done with you. These are my goats – River, Phoenix, Blackberry, Ivy, Josey, Bogie, Mystic, Phineas, Mia, Tonka, Piglet, Styx, LeiLou and Sugar. You can call me Gin.'

'Gin?'

'Yup. Home is where the Gin is.' She winked at Lucy. 'Come on over here and meet my goats. I won't bite.'

She unhooked a hip flask from her belt. 'Gin and tonic, magic water for fun people.' She threw it to Lucy. 'It'll help you relax. Have a swig and come and meet River. He's the friendliest.' She laughed at a joke no one else had heard. 'Sure thing, Mystic.' She winked at the goat closest to us. It was jet black and looking at us in a decidedly unfriendly manner.

Lucy gamely took a big swig from the hip flask before spluttering and coughing. 'There's no tonic in here!'

'My mistake,' Lisette said easily. 'But I promise you,

no great meals start with a salad. Come over here. Let's start your story.'

Lisette took Lucy to the far corner of the field with a black-and-white goat. Emory and I sat down in the field and watched for thirty long minutes while nothing much seemed to happen. Then the black goat came over and tried to pee on Emory. Emory missed the stream only by quickly rolling out of the way.

I snorted with laughter, and he gave me a baleful look. 'If you break my heart, being pissed on by a goat will look like the mildest revenge ever,' I assured him. Gato let out a low growl of agreement.

'I'm not going to break her heart,' Emory assured my parents quickly. 'I love her.' *True.*

I grinned and settled back down against him. 'I love you, too. Maybe after all this is over we could go on holiday. Sun, sand, sea.'

He kissed my neck. 'Sounds good. A honeymoon?' he suggested diffidently.

'Haven't you missed a step?' I asked drily. 'Like a proposal?'

'You know I want us to be formally mated.'

'Sure, but I grew up with Disney. I need romance. I need down on one knee.'

'And a ring?'

I shrugged. 'I can take or leave a ring. It's you I want. But I do have expectations.'

'And those expectations include me getting down on

one knee?'

'Yup. Begging would be nice.'

He shoved his shoulder lightly into mine. 'I don't beg, but I'll definitely ask nicely. You want it to be a surprise, right?'

'That'd be nice. And if you do get a ring, get it yourself. Don't let Summer pick it out.'

'Noted.'

I thought about it for a moment. 'What's your real last name?'

'I don't really have one.'

'No, seriously. On legal documents, what does it say?'

'At the moment, "Elite".'

'Seriously? I thought you were kidding about that.'

'No. It's changed over the centuries – it has to, to keep my immortality from coming out – but now it's Elite.'

'And before you took over the whole creature kingdom?'

'Not the whole of it! For a while I was Jones, and then Smith. But there was a good while when I just didn't have one.'

'Like Cher and Madonna?'

'Sure. Except I can't sing for shit. Don't look at me with that gleam in your eyes. We are not doing karaoke right now.'

'Well, not right now…' I agreed. 'But soon. Maybe on our beach holiday.'

'As long as it's just the birds and the sun who'll be offended,' he offered drily.

'Deal!' We sealed it with a kiss.

'Ugh, spare me,' Lisette drawled as she came over. 'I've given Lucy the basics, the rest she can learn on the fly. Get off my land.'

'Thank you, Lisette,' Emory offered.

'You can take your thanks and shove them where the sun don't shine. You broke my heart, and you've come here parading your new mate. I helped Lucy because it's the right thing to do, but I don't need to see any of you ever again.' She inclined her head towards our car. 'Get gone.'

Amber lingered a moment longer, touched Lisette's elbow and murmured quietly to her. Lisette nodded jerkily, then Amber opened her ever-present bag, pulled on some disposable gloves and took out a Kilner jar. It was filled with a particularly vile shade of green gunk.

We watched as she painted three runes onto Lisette's forehead and one on her sternum. As Amber stepped back, Lisette slumped like a marionette whose strings had been cut. She pulled herself back up slowly, blinking, said something to Amber then turned and walked slowly into her farmhouse. She didn't look back at us.

Amber packed her bag and headed to the car. 'Come on,' she said impatiently, 'stop dawdling. We have things to do.'

CHAPTER 21

'WHAT WAS THAT?' I asked finally. 'Her anger wasn't natural. Someone had cursed her. I broke the curse.'

'Why would someone do that?'

'You're the private investigator, not me. I'm just a witch. I saw no reason to leave her in that state.'

'Can she afford your services?'

'I'll bill the Prime since the curse was undoubtedly aimed at him,' Amber said evenly. 'It was designed to worsen her anger over time. Left unchecked, she'd have killed Emory a long time ago if her will had been weaker. She fought it hard. She must have loved you.'

Emory looked distant and a shade regretful. 'She did.'

Jealousy would have reared its head, except that I could see he was regretful but he wasn't wistful. It was a time that he'd enjoyed, but it was definitely in the past. I could cope with that. He had history; I had to deal with it or I'd tie myself up in knots.

As we set off for home, Lucy turned in her seat to look at Gato. 'Shuffle closer,' she instructed him.

Obligingly, Gato moved closer and hooked his head over her seat. She closed her eyes and touched his obsidian face. Suddenly, her eyes flared open and she turned to me. 'They really are there!' She turned back to Gato. 'Mary! It's so good to hear you after all this time.'

For the next ten minutes, Lucy nodded and punctuated the silence with comments that meant nothing to me: 'Uh huh... Sure... Hmm... Okay... *Really*?'

I was struggling with my impatience, and finally, I couldn't control myself any longer. 'Lucy! What the hell? Please tell me what they're saying.'

'Sorry,' she apologised and reached out to rub my arm. 'Sorry, I just got so wrapped up in their story. So, important highlights. They're all in there together – Isaac, your mum and dad. Together they are Gato. Isaac is still in there, happy as Larry to have his owners with him forever. He's never alone – even when you leave him at the house, he always has company. He's a very simple and lovely hell hound. He really is a cutie.'

She trailed off. 'Sorry, I'm rambling about your dog because your parents have been talking and it's heavy. But you're good with heavy. They were telling me about Faltease. The most important thing is that they're certain he had an accomplice. Faltease did all of the stabbing and Glimmer work himself, but his accomplice did some of the snatching. They got the impression the accomplice was young, maybe a teenager. They never saw him properly because he was always masked and gloved. They said he always wore black.'

I sighed. 'Every fucker in this realm wears black. It's like being at a never-ending funeral.'

'I know! What is it with that? Would it kill them to wear some colour? Black is just not good for my skin tone.'

I grinned at her. Everything looked good with her skin tone.

'Anyway,' Lucy continued seriously, sliding Emory a concerned look, 'the other thing they said is that the accomplice was overheard talking to Faltease about the brethren. Faltease was pleased that the accomplice had managed to infiltrate them so easily. At the time, your parents didn't even know what the brethren was – it was all gobbledygook to them.'

She took a breath. 'They told all of this to the Connection, but it seems to have been suppressed. They always thought it was Lord Gilligan Stone who did the suppressing. As they learnt more about the political landscape of the Other, they realised he was less than warm and fuzzy about the dragons and probably didn't give a crap about the brethren being infiltrated by a kidnapping whack-job.'

Emory's jaw was clenched tight; he was not happy about this new development. Not only did we have a mole, we might have had one for quite some time.

Lucy cleared her throat. 'Besides the bigoted Lord Stone, Skye Forbes is joint number one on their shit list. She was all kinds of dubious back in the day. There were rumours that she didn't enchant the piper correctly so the piper could attend symposium meetings and still pipe the creatures.'

Bingo. 'Emory, did you hear that?' I said. 'My parents heard rumours that Sky didn't enchant the piper properly in the symposium meetings.'

'So the piper could still influence the creatures,' he said grimly.

I nodded. 'If that's true, it suddenly makes the trolls and ogres voting in line with anti-creature movements a lot more sinister.'

Emory raked his hand through his hair. 'The trolls and ogres aren't mine, but I'll reach out to them. This can't be allowed.'

'And if it's true, we need to stop Sky and her rogue piper before the vote about implementing the curtailing measures.'

Emory got his phone out, ready to speed dial, then hesitated.

'Calling Summer?' I asked lightly.

'She normally organises these things,' he said a tad grumpily as we pulled onto my drive.

'Well then, let's clear your PA so she can get back to organising your diary.' I tried not to let any of my jealousy and insecurity show. From Lucy's look, I guess I failed.

Summer was in my front room, laughing with Tom. Tom was smiling but his body language said he was defensive, as if he were cautious about her. Summer's smile cooled as she met my eyes, stood up and extended her hand. 'Jessica Sharp, I presume. What a quaint house you have.'

Summer Lopez had worked for Emory for ten years, but I wouldn't have put her age at a day over mine. Her brunette hair glowed with expensive highlights, and every inch of her screamed rich, from her fitted shirt to her pencil skirt and her oh-so-ridiculously-high heels. Her skin was tanned, her nails were newly painted and her hands glittered with rings. Her cheekbones were high and her eyes were dark beneath perfectly pencilled eyebrows. I struggled not to hate her on sight.

I knew that Lucy had problems with the way other girls reacted to her; being naturally beautiful wasn't the gift that most people assumed it was. Men saw you as unattainable, and other girls hated you before you opened your mouth. Okay, so Summer *had* opened her mouth and she'd been bitchy, but I was going to rise above it, for now. Some part of me recognised her reaction to me as insecurity. Maybe her insecurity and my insecurity could go out on a date.

I smiled my friendliest smile. 'I'm sorry we kept you

waiting. Would you like a drink?'

Surprise flashed in her eyes. 'No, thank you.'

'I have a few questions to ask you. Will you answer them?'

She raised one perfect eyebrow at Emory, who nodded. 'Of course,' she consented.

'Are you loyal to Emory?'

'Of course,' she purred, flashing Emory a smile. *True.*

'Have you passed on sensitive knowledge to any third parties?'

She glared. 'No. Never.' *True.*

'Did you tell anyone where Jake Winters lived?'

'No. Why would I?' *True.*

'Have you told anyone my whereabouts?'

'No.' *True*

'Thank you. You can go.'

She blinked, startled. 'What?'

'You can go,' I repeated.

She stared. 'I'd like to talk to you alone,' she said finally.

'Do you mean Jinx any harm?' Emory asked evenly.

'I'd never harm her physically,' Summer responded carefully. *True.*

Emory frowned. 'That's not what I asked.'

I waved it away. 'Leave us for a moment. It's late. See if you can sort us all some food without Summer's able assistance,' I teased.

'Pizza delivery?' Lucy suggested.

The room emptied until only Summer, Gato and I remained. I didn't draw attention to my parents' decision because I was happy to have some back-up. Summer didn't want to harm me physically, but emotional harm might be on the cards.

Gato leapt up on the sofa next to me and rested his head on my lap. I looked at Summer. 'This is your gig.'

'I've loved Emory for a long time,' she said flatly. 'I accepted ages ago that my feelings are not reciprocated, and I'm working hard at moving on. I have no wish for you to have me fired. I'm an excellent PA, and I love my job, my colleagues.' *True.*

I bit back a comment about which she loved more: Emory or the money. But my mum had taught me better than that, and she was here watching and listening, so I let it slide away. 'Whether you are hired or fired is entirely up to Emory,' I said finally.

'You're his mate. The bonding has already started. Once it settles, you'll be Prima of the dragons. You'll have the power to fire me, if you want to.'

'You're his staff member, not mine.'

'You really mean that?' she asked finally. Her shoulders relaxed. 'You won't fire me just because I … admire Emory.'

I rolled my eyes. 'Summer, have you seen the man? He's an Adonis. If you didn't admire him, you wouldn't be sane. He's sexy, he's rich, he's kind and he's funny. He's so perfect, he makes my teeth ache. But he also snores. He eats a ridiculous amount of food, and sometimes he even burps afterwards. And he really doesn't understand not getting his own way. "No" is a foreign word to him.'

Summer snorted. 'He expects everything to be just so. It's a lot of pressure.'

'I bet it is. I'm glad that's on you and not me. I'm his girlfriend, you're his trusted aide. We both play pivotal but very different roles in his life. As long as you don't try to seduce him, we'll be good.'

Summer hesitated. 'I did try to seduce him a couple of times. He didn't notice.'

I winced a little on her behalf. That would be crushing. 'No more seduction attempts,' I suggested.

'No more, I promise. I don't want a man who doesn't want me.' *True*.

'You deserve a man who wants you. We all do. Don't settle for less than you deserve,' I advised.

She gave me a tremulous smile. 'So we're okay?'

Hell no, I thought, but I nodded, 'We're okay.' I winced internally as my lie detector pinged.

Summer stood and swayed her way to the door. 'I was prepared to hate you,' she admitted.

'Back at you,' I didn't hate her but neither did I trust her. She still loved Emory; I'd have to work at getting over that, like she was working at getting over Emory.

She nodded and left the room to find the others. 'Tom, can you drive me home?' I heard her ask.

Emory ducked his head into the room. 'All okay?'

'Yes, she's clear. Get her onto the trolls and the ogres.'

Emory nodded and went to talk to her.

Lucy walked in with a brew. 'I figured you might need this after hanging out with that Amazonian bitch.'

That made me grin. 'You got anything stronger?'

'Gin?' Lucy said brightly. 'Laughter is the best medicine, but gin is a close second.'

'You spent too long with Lisette.'

'She was nice, albeit a bit pickled. Hopefully now her curse has been lifted, she can start living her life for herself again rather than trying to stave off murderous impulses with copious amounts of alcohol.'

'Yeah, that sucks. This has been a tough day. Lisette loves Emory, Summer loves Emory, I love Emory.'

'I don't love Emory,' Lucy promised. 'He seems nice and all, but he's not my type. But Jinx, remember that Lisette might love Emory, and Summer might love Emory, but Emory loves you.'

Just like that, the tension drained out of me. 'Crazy guy.'

Lucy winked. 'Okay?'

I nodded. 'Okay. Thanks. Maybe you could reach out to Summer – two super-hot girls on the prowl together.

I'd feel happier if she had a boyfriend.'

'I'm on it,' Lucy promised.

Amber popped her head into the room. 'Manners is taking me to a safe house for the night. There's not enough space here for all of us. I'll be back in the morning – don't leave without me.'

'You sure you don't want to stay for pizza and beer?' I asked.

'No. Thank you for the offer but I'm not in a socialising space.'

'Of course. Sleep well, Amber.'

She left abruptly.

'She's a complicated girl,' Lucy commented.

'She certainly is.'

We flicked on the TV and waited for the pizza. Lucy spent the next half hour letting me and my parents converse through her. It was unreal to joke with them again, to have my mum nag me and my dad tease me. Yes, it was unreal – but I'd never been more grateful to have been shoved into this crazy-ass, magical realm where everything was something else. Even my dog.

Lucy frowned a little. 'I don't see how she could.' She muttered, 'but I'll tell her.' She turned to me. 'Your mum says you forgot about your heartbeat.'

My breath caught and suddenly tears filled my eyes. 'I never forgot.' I said, my voice choked, throwing my arms around Gato's neck. 'No matter how hard it was, I never forgot.'

'How can you forget your heartbeat?' Lucy asked curiously. 'It beats, or it doesn't. That's it.'

I managed a watery smile. 'My mum told me, ever since I was little, that she had given me life, and she had given me my heartbeat. And every beat, it told me 'love you', 'love you'.' I said the words rhythmically and tapped my chest in time with my heartbeat as I spoke.

'Shit.' Lucy said, her eyes filling up. 'That's ridiculously cute.'

I nodded. 'I always loved it.' I met Gato's eyes. 'I never forgot my heartbeat, I never forgot you – either of you. It was hard without you, but I always knew I was loved, and I was blessed with that at least.'

Gato nudged my hand and tucked their head around my shoulder in a silent hug.

'They will always love you.' Lucy said softly, so as not to break the spell.

'I know. I love you both too, forever and always.' I whispered back, with my heart feeling so full of love. I was so damn lucky to have this second chance, and I wouldn't forget it.

CHAPTER 22

E MORY HAD COME to bed late and left early. When I reached out and felt the cold, empty sheets next to me, I stirred awake. I blearily checked the time: 5:10 a.m. Who gets up in the dead of winter at 5:10 a.m.? Emory, that's who.

Gato stirred and looked at me reproachfully. 'I know, way too early, right? Can you send me to Other?' I asked. He touched his nose to my forehead and sent me tumbling into the Other realm.

I automatically ruffled his ears in thanks then paused. 'Is that a weird thing to do to your parents?' I asked.

Gato gave a clear headshake, so I ruffled some more.

I dressed in running clothes and stumbled downstairs. Gato reluctantly stretched, his joints popping, and followed me down. Emory was yawning in my kitchen, looking tired.

'Hey,' I greeted him. 'Early start.'

He yawned again. 'The ogres want an early meeting so they can fly under the radar.'

I turned on the kettle. 'Coffee?'

'Please,' he said gratefully. 'I'm not going to survive the day without coffee.'

'As an immortal being, are you saying that coffee is the secret to long life?'

'As an immortal being, I'm saying please pass me some coffee before I get grumpy.'

I grinned. Emory was almost always perfectly turned out, without so much as a hair out of place. It was endearing to see him bleary-eyed and rumpled. One cup of coffee later and his usual sharpness had been restored, but it had been fun to watch the direct correlation between the level of coffee in the cup and his level of suaveness.

'I think I've discovered your secret,' I teased.

He winked. 'Don't tell anyone.'

'It's safe with me.'

Emory's phone buzzed. 'I've got to go. Tom is out front to take me to the ogres. Manners is outside for when you're ready. I've asked him to ride shotgun with you today. Please keep him with you, for the sake of my sanity.'

I liked that he was asking. Also, I wasn't stupid; someone was trying to kill me, albeit incompetently, so I was quite happy to have a highly trained military operative by my side.

I kissed Emory goodbye and he kissed me back with so much enthusiasm that I thought I might persuade him to be late for the ogres. Alas, his sense of duty was too strong. I finished up my coffee solo and tried to work out what to do for the day.

We needed to find Fritz and Ajay, and I wanted to speak to Hes to eliminate her. Cathill was still on my radar, as well. Thinking of the sneaky daemon who'd been instrumental in poisoning Emory's parents, I tapped out a text to Mo, my tech guy. I'd asked him to dig into Cathill but had given him almost no information to go on. Still, a reminder wouldn't go amiss.

The only other things on my to-do were to speak to Bastion and have some more chats with my parents via Lucy. I checked the time: 5:30 a.m. Yuck.

I found Gato's flashing light collar. It was still depressingly dark outside; seeing my pitch-black dog thundering towards you through the darkness without any warning would ruin the constitution of an average man. A flashing collar at least gave some warning that *something* was coming before Gato burst out of the undergrowth.

I did some stretches and turned on my watch to track my run. As promised, Manners was parked up in a black Ford Escape outside my house. I gave him a wave. 'I'm going for a run. You game?'

He slunk out of his car. He was wearing black combats and heavy boots. 'You want to change your shoes?' I suggested.

He gave me an amused look and shook his head. 'If I can't run in these boots, I deserve to be shot.'

He fastened on two guns, one to his ankle and one to his hip. He wasn't concerned about carrying them where they could be seen, which struck me as odd. 'You're not concerned about being stopped?' I asked, gesturing to the weapons.

'Emory has signed me up as your CPO. I have a licence. We're good.'

'CPO?'

'Close protection operative – bodyguard.'

Manners let me go first and he followed, matching my pace. With him behind me, I could almost pretend it was just another run. Gato and I charged through the woods together, scaring only one dog walker. The dog ran away from Gato; I wondered if all dogs were scared of him not because he was a hell hound but because he had three souls inhabiting his body. Who knew?

A brisk five kilometres later, we were back at my house. I showered quickly and dressed for the office. Black jeans, shirt and suit jacket. I'd been neglecting my business, so an early-morning jump on some paperwork seemed like a good idea.

Manners rode shotgun in my Mercedes, while Gato reluctantly agreed to stay at the house and keep an eye on the slumbering Lucy. Lucy was normally an early riser, but perhaps her piping efforts had taken it out of her.

I parked in the underground car park and headed into Volderiss's inner sanctum and the safety of my office. It was just my luck that Verona was manning reception. I gave her a sneer, which she returned, but we both decided it was too early to spar verbally.

Manners took up his post at Hes's desk in the anteroom to my office. Anyone trying to get to me had to get through all bulky 6'4" of him. It was reassuring.

I switched off my worries about Faltease's Fallen, my parents, Jake and the ouroboros, and focused instead on debtors and chasing cheating spouses. I'd had a new request for the latter, and I had evidence of an affair – or at least steamy kisses – only half an hour later. The cheater was sloppy in the extreme. He had two Facebook accounts, one for his wife to see and one for his mistress to see, but he'd used a similar name and the same date of birth, so it wasn't hard to track him down. It was a shame; I charged on a time-spent working basis, so this one was wrapped up in one meagre invoice. Still, the job was done unless the wife wanted to see more, though I doubted she would. Some three-hundred photos at a variety of venues spoke for themselves.

The 9 a.m. test fire alarm blared out, and Manners burst into the room, startling me. 'It's a test,' I explained. 'They do it every day at 9 a.m.'

He nodded and went back to Hes's desk. A minute passed and the alarm still hadn't stopped. I frowned, locked my computer and pushed back from my desk. I went into Hes's office. 'It's normally off by now,' I explained to Manners.

He drew his sidearm and gestured for me to move behind him. 'Hand on my shoulder,' he instructed. It felt like overkill, but what did I know? I obligingly put my right hand on his left shoulder and followed him out.

Verona wasn't at her desk, and a tendril of real worry ran through me. We headed down the stairwell to the underground car park. As we opened the door, thick smoke billowed out.

Verona stepped out of the smoke. As she's one of the undead, she didn't seem concerned about smoke inhalation. 'It's your car,' she announced. 'It's been firebombed. My colleague has already checked the security footage and the cameras have been interfered with. No footage of the bombing. This was professional.' She frowned at me. 'You're screwing up my day. Lord Volderiss is going to be pissed.'

'I'm not thrilled,' I commented drily. I was trying to play it cool but the car had been a present from Emory, a damned expensive present. Even though it was insured, its loss stung. I didn't want a replacement car, I wanted *this* one, the one Emory had given me. And also, I'd quite like not to be targeted by professional firebombers. 'You'll deal with the cops?'

Verona glared. 'Of course. I've got nothing better to

do than to clean up after your messes.'

'That's exactly right,' Nate said firmly, melting out of the shadows and glaring at Verona.

She shrunk back on herself. 'Nathaniel. I didn't see you there.'

'Clearly not. You've been warned about showing Jinx an inappropriate lack of respect. She saved my life – if you treat her badly, you treat me badly. You don't want to treat me badly, do you, Verona?'

She swallowed hard. 'No, Nathaniel. I meant no disrespect to you.'

'Good. Clean this mess up. The Volderiss clan is supposed to be protecting Jinx and this debacle brings shame on us all. Get to the bottom of it. I expect a report on my desk by the end of the day.'

'Yes, sir,' Verona snapped out. She walked towards my car without looking back at me. I felt rather bad for her; to have a dressing down in front of anyone was downright embarrassing, and she and I weren't friends.

Nate stepped closer and hugged me, drawing me away from Manners for a moment of privacy. 'Are you okay?' he asked. He frowned. 'I didn't feel your alarm as strongly as I should have, considering I was only upstairs.'

'I think my bond with Emory has kind of … superseded our bond. It's still there, but it's like background noise. I have to really try to focus on it to feel you.'

Nate nodded. 'Yeah, it's an effort now to locate you.'

'It's a good thing, I guess,' I suggested. 'It's less intrusive.'

'Intrusive or not, I'm still bound to you. You saved me, and I'm oath bound to protect you. I don't regret that.' *True.*

I gave him a light fist bump to the shoulder. 'Me neither. You've become a good friend. But it's still kind of nice not to feel it in my head when you get hot and heavy with Hes.'

Nate's skin warmed slightly.

'I didn't know the undead could blush.' I grinned.

'Anything you can do, we can do better,' he retorted.

'No you can't.'

'Yes we can.'

We both laughed.

Nate's expression grew solemn again. 'I'll get to the bottom of this, Jinx. You have my word.'

I hesitated for a second and then quietly confessed about the other attempts to kill me. Nate let out a low growl. 'That's it. I'm not letting you out of my sight.'

'I appreciate the thought, but Emory's already given me round-the-clock protection.' I nodded at Manners, who was still lurking a few feet away. 'Just do me a favour and see what you can find out about this firebug.'

Nate nodded reluctantly. 'Alright. But if you need me, just call. I'll be there.'

'I know you will.'

Nate gave me one last hug and went to report the fire to his father. Through the smoke I could see vampyrs still tackling my car with extinguishers. I thought about offering my water-elemental skills, but I guessed rivers of water would be hard to explain when the Common cops arrived.

'We're done here,' Manners said firmly, gripping my shoulder and leading me away from the garage. As we left the building though the main entrance, he pulled out his phone and dialled. 'We need extraction,' he barked and then hung up.

'You have terrible phone manners.'

'So you keep saying.'

'Brunch?' I suggested. 'We could go to Moose.'

'Everyone knows you like Moose.' He considered our options. 'This way.' He led me to Dale Street Kitchen and before long we were sitting in front of full-English platters with sausages, bacon and hash browns piled high. That made me all kinds of happy. I know it's not necessarily healthy to eat your way to happy, but after the events of the morning I reckoned I had a free pass to eat my body weight in food. One, I'd been for a run; two, someone had destroyed my £100,000 car. I could eat as much bacon as I wanted to.

Manners phone rang. He answered with silence, listening intently. Finally, he swore. 'Damnit.' He blew out an aggravated breath and looked at me. 'I'm already on duty. You'd better give it to someone else.'

I touched his arm. 'I've got no plans right now. Whatever it is, let's go.' He frowned but he was considering it. 'I'll stick to you like glue,' I promised.

He relented and spoke again into his phone. 'Disregard. I'm on my way.'

We paid our bill. Chris, Emory's driver and pilot, was running the engine on a Maybach outside as we climbed in. 'So, where are we going?' I asked.

'Have you ever heard of the Bebington Hum?' Manners asked. I shook my head. 'Google it,' he advised.

I did so and skimmed a few articles. 'There's a weird hum in Bebington that is heard at all hours. There's been speculation that it's caused by wind farms, helicopters or even aliens, but the local council says it's due to a ship in the dock running its generators.'

'Right. That's the line we've fed the Common realm.'

'And the real cause of the hum?'

'Gargoyles.'

I blinked. 'Sure.'

'Have you ever seen *The Hunchback of Notre Dame*?'

'Sure.'

'Well, it's not the hunchback that likes singing, it's the gargoyles. But the Common realm can't hear it properly.' He grimaced. 'Lucky them – it's an awful racket. The problem is that it can cause aggravation and violence in the Commoners. It puts their teeth on edge, and they don't know why; road rage flares up, domestic violence increases. Gargoyles are part of Emory's ambit, and they've agreed to restrict their singing to the dead of night at 3 a.m. once a month. Not at 10 a.m. Emory's busy with the ogres, so we're going to speak to the gargoyles nicely and tell them to quit.'

'Or else?'

'Or else Emory will withdraw his protection.'

'Who do they need to be protected from?'

'Vampyrs, predominately. Apparently, gargoyles are tasty – the caviar of blood. Occasionally a rogue vampyr gets the idea that they want a midnight snack, and Emory makes sure that doesn't happen.'

'Where are they based?'

'Next to St Andrew's Church. They can't roam too far from church grounds.'

My phone rang. It was Lucy. 'Where are you?' she asked. 'I'm bored.'

'Sorry, I popped in to work. I'm on my way to St Andrew's Church in Bebington to meet some gargoyles.'

'Cool. Gato and I will come, too. Meet you there.' She hung up.

'Uh-oh,' I murmured. Manners raised an eyebrow at me. 'Lucy and Gato are coming along for the ride.'

He sighed. 'More civilians. Great.'

CHAPTER 23

CHRIS PARKED THE car and, at a signal from Manners, strapped on some guns. I guess he was joining the mêlée now that Lucy and Gato were rolling in. The more the merrier.

Chris, Manners and I all looked vaguely professional and badass in black. Lucy rocked up in a pink fluffy coat, pale washed-out jeans and ankle boots that were surely too high to walk in. That made me grin; fashion before practicality. She also had Amber in tow, who was dressed more in line with Other realm's obsession: black skirt, black coat.

'Christ,' Manners muttered.

Lucy gave us a friendly wave, and we walked together towards the churchyard. Before we reached it, I felt a familiar vibration in the soles of my feet. I knew immediately what it was. 'Ouroboros incoming,' I shouted.

We huddled together as Manners and Chris drew their guns and I gathered my intention. This time I didn't hesitate to call fire to my fingertips.

The ground erupted in a spray of mud, gravestones

and bones as the pale-pink body of the giant worm thrust towards the sky. Its mouth was full of razor-sharp teeth, and once again, there was a spray of spikes around its terrifying maw. The gargantuan beast let out an earth-shattering roar.

'That's not an ouroboros,' Lucy protested. 'It's not eating itself.'

'I know.'

'It's bloody huge!' she cried.

It turned its head towards her. 'It also works out your location by sound, so stop yacking and move!' I shoved Lucy, and she proved how well she could run in heels.

We sprinted away from the others as the worm targeted our position, slamming into the ground where Lucy and I had stood mere seconds before. Lucy ran easily over the uneven ground in her fancy boots. 'You don't even go running in trainers,' I complained.

She flashed me a grin. 'I do now. Esme makes me. And besides, I dance.'

We ran towards the relative safety of a tree. Across the way, Manners raised his gun and shot at the ouroboros. It screamed as the bullet bit into it, but it was no more than a flesh wound. We'd need a rocket launcher to take this beast down.

I reached into my suit jacket, expecting Glimmer to have found its way into my pocket. It gave me a moment's pause when I felt nothing but fabric. 'It's not here,'

I said to Lucy.

'What's not?'

'Glimmer.'

She shuddered. 'Don't take this the wrong way, but I'm kind of glad. It's going to be a while before I'm comfortable with the idea of you and that blade.'

Guilt swamped me. 'I'm sorry.'

'Don't be. You saved me. Now save me again. There's a bloody worm after us.'

The ouroboros slammed into the tree we were hiding behind. Its mouth locked around the trunk and pulled, ripping up roots and earth. Lucy and I both tumbled and fell.

'Fuck!' Lucy swore as she crawled out of the hole that the uprooted tree had left behind.

I was focusing on Glimmer. It always appeared when I needed it – which suggested that I *didn't* need it. Glimmer didn't think the ouroboros was our enemy. 'Can you speak to it?' I asked Lucy.

'I don't speak worm!' she retorted, brushing mud from her clothes.

I rolled my eyes. 'Pipe it.'

'Oh. Right. Sure. Pipe that giant mother of a worm.'

Her words made something click. Up and down the body of the worm were nipple-like protrusions; maybe the worm *was* a mother. 'I think it's a mother,' I said. 'It looks like it could be nursing its young.'

'That just means it might see us as food for its babies.'

'I don't think so. Emory said this behaviour is weird for an ouroboros. Remember Lisette?'

'I don't think the worm is going to stand still long enough for Amber to paint some runes on its head.'

'Maybe it will if you can pipe it for long enough. Piping is not just talking to animals, it's also about controlling them.'

'Lisette taught me Piping 101. Controlling giant worms wasn't in the class.'

'You got any other bright ideas?' I threw back.

Lucy huffed. 'I'll need to get close enough to touch it.'

'I'll distract it while you move in.'

'Lucky me.'

'I'll tell Amber first so she can get her supplies ready.'

'That woman was born ready. She's scary.'

I dived left and ran towards the gravestone that Amber was crouching behind. Manners and Chris were still shooting ineffectually at the worm. It had taken to ignoring them, much to Manners' obvious irritation.

I crouched down next to Amber. 'Hey, isn't this fun?'

She gave me a withering look. 'Your definition of fun needs looking at.'

'Each to their own. We need to distract it so Lucy can get close and try to pipe it. I'm wondering if it's been cursed like Lisette was. Can you get stuff ready to break a curse?'

The witch frowned dubiously. 'I'm not sure I've got enough potions on me for a beast of that size, but I'll give it a try. Its behaviour isn't what you'd expect of an ouroboros.' She shook her head. 'We've got some very naughty witches to dig out if they're going around cursing like this.'

'Fun for another day. You ready?' I asked.

She nodded and we stepped out from the gravestone.

I concentrated on pulling flames forwards, making sure they wouldn't burn me or Amber. I grew them until I'd created a wall of fire that I threw over us. As it grew in height, the ouroboros screamed and reared back. Lucy crept forwards, hidden by the flames.

I dropped the wall of fire and created a fireball that I threw at the worm. As the fireball hit it, Lucy also leaned forwards and touched it. It didn't notice as the flame burnt and blistered its skin. The beast screamed and swayed and then stilled.

Lucy's eyes were closed. The rest of us stayed where we were, silent and hopeful. I really didn't want to hurt the worm, not if it wasn't attacking us of its own free will. Slowly it slid back down into the ground, leaving only its head visible.

Amber stepped forwards bravely with her paintbrush and potions. She looked once more at Lucy then started to paint runes on the great beast's head. She got through four separate jars before she had a visible effect. The ouroboros swayed and let out a scream of anguish; slowly its milky-white eyes fixed on us, as if seeing us for the first time.

Lucy opened her eyes. 'We're here to help you, I promise,' she said aloud.

The worm opened its maw and a noise like a purr came out. I felt cautiously optimistic.

Amber smiled. 'The curse is broken. The ouroboros was being controlled alright. It was a compulsion of violence.'

'It's more than that,' Lucy disagreed. 'Whoever did this to her has her babies, her nest of eggs. If she doesn't rampage like she's instructed to, they're going to destroy her eggs.'

Outrage reared up inside of me. Blackmailing a mama through her babies was heinous by any definition. 'Does she know who has them?'

'I'm paraphrasing – her mind is a lot more animalistic. They've got two legs, like us. Two-legs hopes to use her to break the Verdict. If there's enough destruction, it will be hard for the Common to continue accepting our explanation of sink holes and gas explosions. Credulity will only stretch so far.'

Lucy paused, then continued. 'Most of the time, the inspectors are there when she arrives at a specified destination. Two-legs wants the inspectors to look heroic. She doesn't know who has her eggs, not even if they are male or female, because she can't distinguish between us. It's like us not being able to tell the difference between two ants.'

'Well, that's humbling,' Manners muttered.

'Does she know where her eggs are?' I asked.

'No, they were taken and moved. She's grateful that the rage is no longer driving her, but she's still going to follow Two-legs' directions. She was told to come here to attack us. She wasn't told to attack the gargoyles.'

Manners frowned at me. 'You're still the target.'

Emory wasn't going to love this. In all honesty, I wasn't thrilled either. I turned to Chris. 'Do you have a tracking device in your car?'

He nodded, went to the Maybach and opened a suitcase in the boot of the car. He rifled around for a few moments and came back with a hefty-looking gun loaded with something red and flashing. 'I've put it in a tranq gun,' he said. 'We can use that as the delivery method.'

'Lucy, can you ask if she'll let us track her? Until we can secure her eggs, we can make sure we're first on scene when she's wreaking havoc.'

A moment later Lucy nodded. The ouroboros lowered her head and opened her mouth wider.

'Hide it behind a tooth if possible,' I instructed.

Manners took the gun from Chris and stepped forwards. He raised the tranq gun and shot the tracking device into the worm's mouth. She let out a rumble of complaint but otherwise didn't fuss, then she closed her great mouth and bobbed her head slightly. She gave one last roar for good effect and disappeared back into the ground.

CHAPTER 24

M ANNERS LEFT THE rest of us outside in the wasteland that we'd made and headed into the church to speak with gargoyles. I'd like to say he was protecting us, but I think by now he was just sick of the circus that followed in our wake. His cleanly run military operations tended to go into a total shambles when I came along for the ride. Clearly, he wasn't as well versed in the 'expect the unexpected' school of thought as he needed to be if he was going to carry on hanging out with me.

While we waited for Manners, I walked away from Lucy and Amber and called Bastion. The phone stopped ringing and I spoke into the silence. 'I need to talk to you in person. I know you killed Jake. I *liked* Jake. I know you're an assassin. but he was my parents' friend, like you. It's hard to wrap my head around the fact that you're both an assassin and my parents' friend. But they'd like to see you, I'm sure, and I need to talk to you. Please? I know you care about me. This is important. I need your help.'

The silence stretched out. I pulled out my trump card. 'Someone's trying to kill me. And I think whoever it is hired you to kill Jake.'

'I'll be around,' Bastion said simply and hung up. No when or where, just that he'd be around. The men in my life had become infinitely more annoying since I'd joined the Other realm. Of course, before I'd joined it I hadn't *had* any men in my life, so it still felt like an improvement.

I bit my lip and considered my options. I couldn't have Amber with me when Bastion arrived so I needed to distract her, get her somewhere away from me.

I re-joined her and Lucy. 'When we're done here, Manners and I will need to update Emory about the ouroboros. Time is ticking, though, and we need to find out who is going around cursing people. My gut says Sky Forbes. I'm sure she's up to her neck in it, but Amelia Jane was the one who put faulty runes on my house. Are you two up for questioning her while I cross Hes off our suspect list?'

Lucy's eyebrows shot up. 'Why is Hes on our suspect list? She's a sweet as sugar eighteen year old, not a conspiracy hound.'

'She knew where Jake lived,' Amber explained. 'Someone gave that information to Jake's killer.' Her voice was tight.

'Gato? Can you ride with Lucy and Amber, help keep

them safe?' I asked. 'Battle cat on Amelia if you need to.' Gato barked an affirmative and wagged his tail.

Amber got out her phone and rang someone. 'Get me a location for Amelia Jane. Keep it to yourself.' She hung up.

'We don't need Gato if you want him with you,' Lucy offered. 'Esme and I are ready to kick ass if we need to.'

I blinked a bit at that. On some level I knew that Lucy was a werewolf, but I hadn't seen her and Esme in action so it was hard to remember that my accountant friend was also a ferocious wolf. However, a werewolf's transformation could take upwards of five minutes, whereas Gato's was almost instantaneous, and even in his more placid form, he was deadly. I wanted the girls safe.

'No, it's okay. You take Gato. I'd feel better if you had back-up. I'm only going back home, and I have Manners.'

Amber's phone vibrated. 'I've got a location. Let's go.'

Lucy leaned forwards to whisper to me. 'Life is so much fun now we're magical!' She beamed as she headed back to her car with Gato and Amber in tow.

I couldn't help but agree; life now was fun – crazy, but fun. I texted Emory to keep him in the loop: *The ouroboros popped up. It was cursed like Lisette. Amber broke the curse but it's still going to keep popping up. Someone is holding its eggs hostage.*

A moment later I got a response: *10-4. It looks like the ogre symposium member has been controlled by the symposium piper. The witch responsible for ensuring that the piper couldn't pipe was Sky Forbes.*

She's been on our shit list for a while, I responded.

Good to have it confirmed. Trying to get in to speak to the trolls, but it's slow going.

I grimaced a bit at that. Everything with the trolls was slow going; they rumbled and ambled at what seemed to be an agonisingly slow pace to us mere mortals.

Keep in touch. X

Stay safe, Jess. x

I didn't tell him about my little car fire, or that the gargoyles seemed to have been used to bring us to a place where we could be attacked by the ouroboros. Some news is best delivered in person, like telling someone you're pregnant or admitting that someone has tried to kill you again.

Manners emerged from the church. 'Where are the others?'

'Amber, Lucy and Gato are going to question one of the witches.'

He considered me for a moment. 'And what are we going to be doing that you wanted them out of harm's way?'

I grinned. 'You're really getting to know me.'

'Let's plait each other's hair next,' he suggested drily.

Chris laughed then tried to play it off as a cough as Manners glared at him.

'I've asked Bastion to come and visit.'

'Bastion, the deadly assassin who killed Amber's lover Jake?'

'Yup. That one.'

Manners sighed and looked at Chris. 'There just isn't enough manpower around to keep you safe.'

'Bastion won't hurt me. He thinks of me like a niece.'

Manners disagreed. 'He would hurt anyone for the right fee.' *True.*

It was a sobering thought. I was fairly certain that Manners was wrong, even though he believed he was right. I thought of the love that I'd felt when Bastion had hugged me. No, he wouldn't hurt me. 'He won't hurt me,' I insisted. 'Let's go. I don't want to make him wait.'

'What time is he coming?'

'He didn't say, so I'm guessing that means his ETA is imminent.'

'Where are we meeting him?'

'He didn't say, so it'll be at my house.'

Manners huffed. 'He doesn't say much.'

'No. It adds to the air of mystery,' I joked.

'No kidding.'

We piled into the Maybach and Chris took us home. Manners sat in the back with me and filled me in about his chat with gargoyles. The gargoyle who'd been singing was their equivalent of a teenager; he'd been paid to sing at that particular time by some 'Connection dude'. The only thing he could be sure of was that it was definitely a guy. 'Apart from that, it was dark figure. I just saw the money,' he'd said.

Manners told me that the gargoyle was going to be punished appropriately for breaking their rules; the little guy would have to stand in daylight for a solid week, still as a statue and unable to move. It seemed harsh to me, but a lot of the things in the Other were harsh. It wasn't my place to judge, just to survive.

Chris parked up and Manners told him to come inside with us. I guessed he really was worried about Bastion. I unlocked the front door and started into my house, then paused as I saw the griffin lounging on my sofa.

He was lying down like Gato did, lion legs spread out, eagle body sitting upright with his claws resting casually on the sofa's arms. The thought that the deadly assassin was once again sitting on Hes's sex sofa amused me. My next thought didn't. 'The house was locked securely and it's runed up to the hilt,' I sighed. 'You shouldn't have been able to get in.'

'So?' Bastion responded calmly.

'Yeah. Money well spent. Do you want a brew?'

Bastion inclined his great head. 'Yes, please.'

I went into the kitchen to make some tea while Manners and Chris stayed with Bastion. Chris was a little wild-eyed. I set four mugs on the tray as well as some biscuits, then carried the tray in and set it down carefully. 'Milk? Sugar?'

'Milk, no sugar. Thank you,' Bastion replied politely.

'Manners? Chris?' They both shook their heads.

I paused before handing Bastion's tea to him. 'How does it work with talons and beak?'

'It doesn't,' Bastion responded. He shimmered and a moment later the man I recognised sat there, complete with black combats, black T-shirt, black boots and a black attitude.

Manners swore long and loudly. 'Hi, Greg,' Bastion said, a small smirk tugging at his lips.

'For fuck's sake, I've known you for eight years, Sam,' Manners groaned.

'The Prime felt it was need-to-know only.'

'As deputy head of his security, I would argue that I very much needed to know that the deadliest assassin in recent times is masquerading as one of ours.'

'Thank you.'

'It wasn't a compliment, Sam,' Manners growled.

Bastion took a sip of his tea and turned to me. 'Jessica.'

'Bastion,' I said. 'Or Sam. Do people call you Bast? I think Bast would be cool.'

He fixed me with steely eyes and I remembered the fear he had once inspired in me. I smirked. 'Not going to work, Bast. You love me.'

His lips tipped up fractionally, the tiniest of movements, but I recognised it was what passed as a smile for him.

'How's your daughter?' I asked.

'You have a daughter?' Manners exploded.

'Oops, sorry,' I said.

'I'm not telling *you* any secrets,' Bastion sighed, looking at me.

'I'm so good at keeping secrets!' I protested. 'But here's a tip – tell the person that it *is* a secret.'

'Noted. You said your parents would be here.'

Manners looked at me sideways. 'Your parents are dead.'

I glared at Bastion. 'Now who's giving away secrets?'

Bastion sipped his tea. 'Oops.'

Despite myself I grinned. He was teasing me, and it was nice. I drank my tea and ate a couple of biscuits; I wasn't in a hurry, and Bastion didn't seem to be either. To pass the time, I filled him in on the numerous attempts at taking my life – or at least scaring me.

'I checked. There isn't a contract out on you anywhere.' *True.*

'The fire had a professional vibe.'

'It wasn't an assassin but it could have been a firebug. If they were really trying to kill you, the faulty fire alarm would have been co-ordinated with a fire in your office, and your escape route would have been blocked. Not to mention that I'd know that there was a contract out.'

'Maybe they can't afford to pay.'

'There are all sorts of fee structures,' Bastion explained.

'Payment plans for death. Nice.'

'Shirdal has good commercial sense.' *True.*

'That drunkard runs the business side of things?' I asked.

Bastion smiled. 'That *drunkard* runs the whole griffin clan.' *True.*

I took a sip of tea to cover my surprise. It felt like something Emory could have mentioned. 'And Emory is your Prime?' I asked.

Bastion nodded.

'But why does a clan of deadly assassins need protection from Emory?'

'We are very few in number, and his reach is far wider than ours. Shirdal has been … unstable these last few years since giving up death, and Emory felt that a more secure leadership was in order. He's not been an unreasonable Prime,' Bastion admitted grudgingly.

I felt a prickle of guilt. Shirdal had given up dealing in death and mayhem for seven years, until he'd helped rescue me from Ronan's clutches. Then his seven-year clean period went out the window as he killed and maimed dozens of Ronan's henchmen. I cleared my throat. 'You ready to get down to business?' I asked.

'I'm always ready for business.'

'Er, my business, not yours.'

The slight smile flashed again, and Bastion inclined his head.

I stood up. 'You remember how this works?'

'You touch me and divine the truth.'

'That's the one.'

I needed skin-to-skin contact, so I sat next to him on the sofa. I let the ocean recede and I prepared myself to divine. Audrey's book had talked about the importance of anchoring yourself on something physical, so I held my cooling mug in one hand and reached out to touch Bastion's cheek with the other.

I gathered the intention within me. I needed to know who had hired him to kill Jake. I *needed* to know.

Bastion was in an office that I recognised straight away. It was light and airy, with a solitary plant that was quietly dying in the corner. Sky sat behind the desk, a false smile painted on her face. 'We have an old problem we need you to fix,' she said calmly, like she was talking about a leaky drain.

'Here, you asshole,' sneered another voice that I recognised.

Zachary Stone. My stomach plummeted. Stone?

Stone stepped forwards and passed Jake Winter's file to Bastion. He was careful to make sure his skin didn't touch Bastion's, and his face was filled with a quietly controlled rage. He hated that he was working with Bastion, breathing the same air as the bastard who had killed his father.

Bastion took the file, coolly ignoring Stone's vitriol. He thumbed through it quickly, lingering only over address and photos. Amber featured in the photos, coming and going from Jake's house. There was no sign of me; they must have been taken later on the day that I visited.

'Make it look natural,' Stone ordered. 'We all know you're good at that. We're not ready for an uprising yet.'

Sky smirked. 'Soon enough.'

Bastion slid a piece of paper to Sky. 'My payment terms.'

She barely flicked her eyes at it. 'Agreed. Arrange termination within forty-eight hours. No more loose ends. And I invoke the confidentiality clause. Not a word to anyone of the target, not a footnote in a file, not even to the precious Shirdal.'

Bastion nodded again. He paused and then, when it was clear that no further information would be forthcoming, he left.

The vision ended and started to loop. I focused on the feel of the porcelain mug in my hand and felt its smoothness. I blinked as the living room came back into focus. 'Fuck,' I said aloud.

Bastion nodded. 'Indeed.'

CHAPTER 25

H ES CHOSE THAT moment to come home. She paused in the hallway and looked at us. 'Are you okay?' she asked me. 'Nate said you were alarmed. He was going to head off, but he said he'd stay outside in case you need him.'

I did my best to smile. 'Fine, thanks, just a little surprised,' I decided it was best to get straight to the point. 'Listen, while you're here, can I ask you some questions?'

She looked surprised and smiled uncertainly. 'Sure.'

'Are you loyal to me?'

'Absolutely,' Hes confirmed fiercely. *True.* If she found the question weird, she didn't show it.

'Have you passed on sensitive knowledge to any third parties?'

'Um … no.' *True.* Her tone this time showed she was wondering what the heck was going on.

'Did you tell anyone where Jake Winters lived?'

'No! Of course not.' *True.* Her tone was vehement but thankfully not offended. I didn't want to upset her, and I really didn't think she was involved.

'Have you told anyone about my whereabouts?' I asked.

'No, never.' *True.*

'Sorry, we had to be sure.'

Hes blinked. 'Sure of what? What's going on?'

'We have a leak, and we're trying to find out where.'

'Not me! I'd never betray you, I have a total bro-mance going on with you – girl-mance. I think you're the best.' *True.*

I smiled distractedly. Something she'd said had struck a chord within me. A bromance. My chest tightened as I suddenly remembered the last time I'd thought about a bromance: it had been Stone. And Ajay.

Stone left to use the bathroom, and I took advantage of the moment alone with Ajay. 'I know Stone trusts you, but I don't know you. Will you give me your oath that you'll keep my truth-seeking abilities to yourself?'

Ajay nodded. 'I'm Stone's man. If he trusts you, I trust you. I give you my oath. As we will it, so shall it be.' True.

Ajay was Stone's man, not Emory's. Shit. Well, it seemed like I'd found the leak.

Hes was looking at me with concern. 'Are you okay?'

I forced a tight smile. 'I've been better. I know I asked you to come, but things are kind of hairy right now. My car got firebombed.'

'Oh no!'

'I'm doing better than my car. Can you stay with Nate

for a few more days? Just so I know you're safe? And avoid the office?'

'I guess I can do that.' She cast a look at Bastion, Manners and Chris. 'Are you sure you're okay?'

'I'm fine. This is my protection detail.'

Her shoulders relaxed. 'Oh. Great. You want me to look after Gato for a few days? In case things get hectic?'

'That's kind of you to offer, but I hate to be apart from him.'

'I get that. Well, I'll let you get on. Give me a call when we can hang again.'

'Absolutely.'

'I'll just grab some fresh clothes. It's a good thing Nate is still waiting out front.' And it was. I could feel his concern at my emotions, and I did my best to reassure him. I wanted him and Hes safe, not in the middle of whatever was going on.

After Hes had collected her things, she jogged downstairs and called out a farewell. The front door slammed shut behind her. There was a long silence before anyone spoke.

'What did you learn from Bastion?' Manners asked impatiently, ignoring the man himself.

'Stone and Sky hired Bastion. And Ajay is working for Stone.'

Manners froze. 'Ajay? You're sure?'

I nodded. 'Pretty damned sure. Ajay once swore to

me he was Stone's man and it rang true. Emory and I went to bust Ronan's lab, and an elemental called Franklin found us super-fast. Ajay was one of the few who knew we were going there. It's all adding up, and it's not looking good for Ajay. Which sucks, because I really liked him.'

Manners let out a sharp breath of relief. 'Good enough for me.' He pulled out his phone and punched in a number. We heard the beep for the answer machine. 'I know you're hiding out. Ajay is our leak. Come out and talk to me, Fritz. We need you.'

Bastion stood up and all eyes swung towards him. 'I'll be around,' he said to me.

'Thanks for coming.' And for pulling the rug out from under my feet again.

Bastion nodded and left. He took taciturn to a whole new level.

I excused myself and went to the privacy of my bedroom. I dialled Emory and hoped he was still cooling his heels trying to see the trolls. 'Hey, Jess,' he greeted me, his warm baritone washing over me. It made me feel more relaxed.

'Hey. The shit is hitting the fan,' I said. 'I've got good news and bad news.'

'Bad news first.'

'Ajay is our leak.'

'Fuck.'

'Yeah.'

'He was the one that sicced Benedict on us?'

'Yeah.'

There was a beat of silence while we both remembered all too vividly Emory's kidnap and torture. It hadn't been pleasant, to say the least, and Emory still had the occasional nightmare. Ajay was at least partly responsible, though it was still hard to believe.

'The good news?' Emory asked finally.

'There's some more bad news first.'

Emory sighed. 'Hit me.'

'Stone seems to have gone fully dark. Sky and Stone ordered the hit on Jake.'

'I never liked Stone anyway.'

'Yes, you are the supreme judge of character, and I got it wildly wrong,' I said, a tad annoyed.

'I got Ajay wrong,' Emory said softly. 'He's been on my team since I became Prime. He was one of the first wizards that I turned into a spy ... and all this time...' He cut off.

'You want the good news?'

'Yeah, some good news would be good.'

'Hes is all good, and we've called Fritz to tell him to come in. I'll question him, just to be sure – fool me twice and all that – but with Ajay in the firing line, Fritz is probably innocent.'

'I hope so. If I'm wrong about Fritz too then I'll quit.

Fritz is … special. You'll like him.'

'I liked Ajay,' I grumbled.

'Lesson learned. Liking and trusting aren't the same things.'

'No, they're not,' I agreed. In the past few months I'd started to open myself up to trusting people. I grimaced; that was going to backslide now.

'This is just a bump in the road, Jinx. Don't let it upset you. Don't give them that power over your emotions.'

'Yeah.' Easier said than done. I searched for a topic to move us away from emotional territory. 'We've got to find those ouroboros' eggs. The poor thing is being blackmailed with threats to her children's safety. She must be so scared.'

'You want me to come home?' Emory asked immediately.

It warmed me to think that home meant by my side.

'No. I'm good, honestly. Just a bit shaken by it all. But you need to warn the trolls about the piper. We need as many people on side as possible, and we need to know how far this piper has gone. I think all of this – the spider, the firebomb – it's just a smokescreen to keep us from realising they're trying to rig the votes to curtail the creatures' freedom. Your job is way more important than mine right now.'

There was a heavy silence. 'Firebomb?' Emory said finally.

'Oh. Didn't I mention that?' I said breezily. 'Someone firebombed my Merc while we parked at my offices.'

'No. You didn't mention that,' he said, his voice tight.

'It must have slipped my mind. Anyhoo, I'm fine and Manners was with me, and he went full military on my ass and went into CPO mode and everything. I'm fine.' I drew a breath.

'When you say "I'm fine" repeatedly, it makes me worry that you're not. I should have felt you being upset via the bond but I was too focused on the ogres. I'm sorry.'

'Honestly, I have insurance. I'm not that upset. Don't let it ruin your day. The positive thing is, we know who we're fighting now, and we even know why. So really, this has been a good day.'

'I still haven't got in to see the Elder. I'm sorry, I don't think I'll be there to tuck you into bed tonight.'

'I'll be lonely,' I said in my best seductive voice. It sounded to me like I needed a cough sweet. I grimaced and cleared my throat. I'm really not good at soppy. Or seductive. Thankfully, Emory still seemed to think I was just fine. 'Anyway, I'd better go. Speak soon. I love you, Emory.'

'I love you too, Jess.'

We hung up and I dialled Lucy. 'Hey, Luce, how did it go with Amelia?'

'It hasn't,' Lucy said, sounding grumpy. 'Amelia Jane

has vanished. Poof. We're at one of the local covens. Amber is going to stock up on her potions and re-charge, and tomorrow we'll try a tracking spell to find Amelia. We're going to spend the night here. You okay for us to keep Gato?'

'Sure. Just take care of him – them.'

'Always.'

'Keep me in the loop. Love you, Luce.'

'Love you, Jess.'

I rang off and heard the front door slam shut downstairs. Apparently I had a visitor.

CHAPTER 26

I WALKED INTO my lounge to see Manners giving a skinny Black British boy a desperate hug. 'I'm so glad to see you, kid,' Manners murmured to him.

The kid – I guessed he was Fritz – nodded against Manners' shoulders and stayed in the embrace. 'I thought you didn't trust me.' His voice was inches from tears.

'Of course I trust you! I never doubted you, kid.' *Lie.* Manners met my eyes and grimaced then looked away in shame. He cleared his throat and stepped back from the man-hug. 'Fritz, I want you to meet our soon-to-be Prima, Jessica Sharp.'

Fritz whirled around, excited. He was in a tracksuit – black, of course – and it made him look young. I put his age at about eighteen, maybe younger. His hair was shaved short, and his cheekbones were high. He was going to grow up to be a real looker.

'Nice to meet you Fritz.' I smiled.

He ducked his head shyly and leaned back into Manners. 'My real name is Jerome but everyone calls me Fritz.'

I studied him. 'What do you prefer?'

'Well, I never had anybody give me a nickname before, so Fritz is pretty special.'

'It is. I'd love to call you Fritz and you can call me Jinx. That's my nickname.'

He brightened. 'Cool. So are we friends now?'

'That'd be nice. Are you a dragon or brethren?'

He giggled. 'Neither. I'm a terrible wizard. I can hardly summon the IR to float a ball. Apparently I lack focus.'

Manners bristled. 'You're brilliant, Fritz. I've never seen anyone so focused. You ignore those wizards.'

Fritz beamed at Manners, hero worship in his eyes. 'Sure thing, Greg.' He turned to me. 'The Prime found me when I was a youngster running in the streets. He sent me to school but I didn't like it, so he sent me to a better school where I learnt about coding and hacking. I liked that. I like patterns. I finished school early and he let me work for him and all the creatures.'

I raised an eyebrow. 'You know about the Prime Elite thing, huh?'

'Oh sure. When the Prime wants someone to work out he's the boss of a few different types of creature, he gets them to kneel and bow and stuff, and then even the slowest of us figures it out eventually.'

'Does he now?' I said flatly. I vividly recalled Jack Fairglass kneeling in the rocks at Hilbre island.

Fritz nodded, hands tapping on his thighs. 'Uh-huh.

As long as you figure it out, that doesn't break the geas because you haven't been *told* – you've kind of been *shown*. Clever, huh?'

'Clever,' I agreed. I guess I should have felt flattered that I'd worked it out after only one other species had genuflected to Emory. I'd hate to be thought of as slow on the uptake. My tummy rumbled. 'Anyone fancy pizza for dinner?'

Chris stood. 'I'll stand watch for the first portion of the night. Bring me pizza when it's here.'

Manners nodded. 'Deal.'

'I love pizza,' Fritz said excitedly. 'Especially barbeque. Can we get a barbeque pizza? With sweetcorn?'

I saw why Manners often called him 'kid'. Fritz was enthusiastic and warm, like a puppy you wanted to look after. 'Sure. I like sweetcorn. We can do that.'

I ordered pizza for us all. We were watching some TV when my phone buzzed. It was Mo. *Got a location for your Cathill. Credit card was also used at a nearby café this morning.* The address followed.

I sat up straight. 'Guys, we've got a potential address for Cathill.'

Fritz gestured to my phone. 'Can I see that?' I passed it to him. 'Why didn't I find that?' he muttered, frowning. He reached down to a black bag and pulled out two laptops. He turned them both on and started typing frantically.

'He's gone now,' Manners commented. 'He'll surface again for food or when he's figured out whatever's bugging him.'

'He's a bright kid.'

'Yeah, he is. He'll find what he's looking for, he always does.'

'We don't need him focusing on Cathill right now. We need more info on Ajay, Stone and Sky,' I pointed out.

Manners eyed Fritz dubiously. 'Once he's sunk, it can be hard to get him to surface.'

I called Fritz's name a couple of times but he blanked me. He was in the zone.

We went back to the TV as we waited for pizza or for Fritz to surface, whichever happened sooner. Finally the food arrived. I brightened; I could do anything with pizza, including breaking a kid's trance.

I tipped the delivery guy, handed one to Chris and took the rest into the lounge where Fritz was still frantically clicking away. I waved a slice of barbeque chicken pizza under his nose. Absentmindedly he tried to take it, but I moved it away each time until he looked up in irritation and met my eyes.

'Hey, Fritz,' I said. 'I need you to ignore the Cathill thing for now. What we need is a location for some ouroboros eggs.'

Fritz blinked a couple of times. 'The eggs will need to

be kept cool, so you'll need a place with a basement or cellar.'

'That's what I need you to dig for. A place with a basement or cellar, linked to Cathill, Ajay Venn, Zachary Stone or Sky Forbes. I guess you could look into Amelia Jane, too. Oh, and a company called Linkage LLP.'

Manners raised an eyebrow at that.

'It's a company that the Connection uses to buy their black-op sites,' I explained.

'Nice.'

Fritz was already back to typing frantically. I grabbed some pizza and passed Manners one of the other boxes. 'After we're fed, you want to check out the location on Mo's text with me?'

'If I say no, you're going anyway,' he stated resignedly.

'Yup.'

'You're a pain in my ass, Toots.' *True.*

'You'd be bored without me. Admit it.'

'Being a military man is ninety percent being bored and ten percent thinking you're about to die.'

'Let's go ten percent together.'

Manners barked a laugh despite himself and shook his head. He checked the time. 'The Prime is still with the trolls. He's locked down with no communications in or out. So yes, I'll come with you – but if something happens to you, he's going to kill me.'

I rolled my eyes. 'Don't be a drama queen. Nothing is going to happen. We're going to peek in Cathill's windows, that's all. Besides, Emory isn't my boss.'

'He's *my* boss,' Manners retorted dryly. 'Try not to get me dead or fired.'

'You just don't know how to have fun.'

After we'd consumed a good amount of pizza, we both went to the bathroom – always essential in preparing for a stakeout. I grabbed my winter jacket and lock picks, and headed out to Chris and Manners. I could see that Manners was torn; he wanted to take Chris with us as back-up, but he wanted to keep Fritz safe.

I made the call for him. 'You stay here with Fritz,' I instructed Chris. 'We're going for a drive.'

He nodded. '10-4'.

Manners glared. 'I give the orders around here, Toots.'

'Sure – but you were going to give the same order, right?'

He opened his mouth ready to deny it, but closed it knowing I'd sense a lie. 'Let's go,' he growled.

I let him drive to soothe his ego but also so he could do some evasive driving if we needed it. After all, someone was still after me. Then I climbed into the passenger seat, plugged Cathill's supposed address into the Sat Nav and hit go.

CHAPTER 27

WE PARKED ON Aigburth Drive, a few houses down from Cathill's place. It was 8:30 p.m. and dark, but we could still see his property from our position.

The house was spectacular. It was a whacking great mansion overlooking Sefton Park, cream stone with red fascia boards and arched windows. It looked very fancy, and it was a stone's throw away from the infamous Lark Lane, home to a bunch of independent food joints. It was trendy with a capital T. It shouldn't pay so well to be the bad guy, I thought bitterly.

Luckily, we were far enough away from the bargoers not to raise eyebrows in our jeans and jackets and without a spray tan or fake eyelash between us. I pictured Manners with a spray tan and false eyelashes and grinned; they'd look good with his pink hair.

He eyed my grin with suspicion then turned his attention back to Cathill's property. We watched silently for a half an hour. It was just hitting 9 p.m. and there were no movements and no lights. I didn't know anything about daemons so I had no idea of their bedtime, but it just didn't seem right that a daemon would be in bed for 8:30 p.m.

'Do you reckon he's sleeping?' I broke the silence.

'Daemons don't sleep. It's one of the reasons they don't stay in a host for too long because lack of sleep makes the host break down.'

I considered that. 'Cathill was a vampyr before he was subsumed, so maybe he doesn't need sleep. He was the local vampyr leader but he's been out of politics since the whole debacle with Mrs H. After that he was officially in the Connection's bad books, so he had to step back but not down. Nate tells me his clan is being run by his second, someone called Morris.'

'I know Morris.' Manners' tone suggested he had nothing good to say about him.

'Bosom buddies?' I teased lightly.

'He used to be one of the biggest dragon hunters around. He claimed nineteen kills over the decades, some of them just younglings.'

I lost my good humour. Jeez Jinx: open mouth, insert foot. 'That's horrible. Sorry.'

'There's a lot of bad blood between dragons and vampyrs. Nate is new, and has spent most of his life with the Connection in existence, so maybe he didn't personally hunt us down like dogs. But there's going to be a lot of resistance to the Prima being friends with a vamp.'

'Politics don't dictate my friendships,' I said firmly.

Not long ago I hadn't had all that many friends; Nate had earned his stripes and proved his worth. He'd leapt into danger to help me. I vividly remembered the bloodbath at Rithean Castle when Nate had come with back-up to rescue me from Ronan. As it happened, I hadn't needed rescuing because Shirdal had pretty much destroyed all of our enemies in a terrifying and sobering display of strength and unbridled violence. But Nate had come – and he'd even come when Emory was in danger. He and I had skydived into a castle full of our enemies. It mattered.

The silence hung heavily between us until the tension was too much for me. I was used to doing stakeouts alone or with Gato, not with a brooding Manners next to me. I unbuckled my seatbelt. 'Come on,' I said as I opened the door.

'What are you doing?' Manners hissed. 'We're here to observe.'

'Let's observe closer.'

The cold was biting after the warmth of the car, and I slipped my hands into my pockets. I encountered my lockpick set in one pocket and cold hard metal in the other. Glimmer. Oh damn. Shit was about to go down.

'Have you got a weapon?' I whispered to Manners.

He snorted derisively and didn't answer. I took that to mean, 'Yes, lots of weapons.' I hoped I was right.

We crept closer to the property and walked onto the driveway, keeping low and clinging to the shadows. It would have been handy to have Emory or Nate there to phase us through those shadows.

We inched closer to the property until we could peer in at the windows. The building was old and tall – it looked like it had three floors and a basement. That was definitely somewhere eggs could be kept. Manners swore under his breath. He'd come to the same conclusion. 'Stay here,' he ordered.

Some bodyguard he was. He left me crouched in the darkness while he walked the perimeter, peering through the windows, then he disappeared around the back of the house. I waited for a long ten minutes before impatience got the better of me.

I tiptoed around the back and bumped straight into Manners. 'The house looks empty,' he breathed. 'I'm going in to clear the rest of the property and check the basement.'

'I'm coming with you.' I held up a hand to forestall his argument. 'I don't have any weapons, and I'm a sitting duck out here.' *Lie.* 'I'm safer with you.' That at least was true.

He gestured with his head, and I followed him into the house. I didn't know if he'd picked the locks or if the back door had been open. I hadn't seen a shitload of runes; either they were hidden or Cathill was confident in his ability to kill anyone foolish enough to enter his space. That was something fun to think about as I crept across his threshold.

Creeping about on creaking floorboards made me wince as we searched the property floor by floor. The rooms we peered into were opulent and fancy, and everything was immaculate. Either Cathill had a cleaner or he wasn't living there. We didn't do a thorough search, just a quick check to ensure that we were the sole occupants. So far so good. But Glimmer was weighing heavily in my pocket.

We came back downstairs and looked in the kitchen. There was food in the fridge, fresh bread on the side. A warning tingle flared in my gut. Someone was definitely living here.

When we found the basement stairs, Manners took point. I drew Glimmer from my pocket and held it loosely by my side. I'd done martial arts regularly from an early age but, when it came to knife fighting, Glimmer had a mind of its own. It didn't need me to direct it.

Our eyes had largely adjusted to the dark. The basement door swung open silently, and we crept down the steep stairs, tension high. The area was huge and cavernous, and I could see the outline of what looked to be scores of human-sized eggs. Bingo. We moved closer to them, still squinting in the dark.

Abruptly I remembered that I was a freaking wizard. I summoned the IR and willed myself to see in the dark. 'Vision,' I murmured. It was like a light switch had been thrown. Suddenly I could see perfectly – which was handy because now I could see the jet-black werewolf that was stalking towards us on silent paws.

'Werewolf!' I shouted a warning at Manners and raised Glimmer defensively. The werewolf let out a growl and started to run. I was about to summon fire to scare him when I suddenly realised that I couldn't do that without risking barbecuing the ouroboros eggs.

By the time I'd thought that through, the werewolf was nearly upon me. Luckily Manners' thought processes weren't nearly so stagnant. He drew his gun and shot the wolf as it thundered towards us. He shot it once, twice, three times – and it kept on coming.

As it leapt towards me, I held out Glimmer as a pathetic last defence. Glimmer, of course, was not in the least pathetic, and it flashed through the air towards the heart of the beast.

Manners wasn't done. From under his jacket he withdrew a machete-like blade that had been hidden down his spine. As the werewolf flew towards me, Manners' blade flew down, neatly severing the werewolf's head from its shoulders. Headless, the beast continued moving towards me, and I stumbled and fell with its weight on top of me, its heart skewered on Glimmer.

I hit the ground with an oomph and struggled to push the corpse off me. Manners helpfully tossed it aside like it didn't weigh 150 kilos. He raised an eyebrow at

Glimmer and put on a falsetto voice. 'I'm coming with you. I don't have any weapons of my own, I'm a vulnerable maiden.'

'Sitting duck,' I corrected. I shrugged. 'I fibbed.'

'No shit,' he said flatly.

He pulled me up, and we both looked down at the hairy corpse. Its blood was pooling around it and I had a good amount of it on my clothes. 'Well, I think we found the person who was eating the nice bread,' I commented.

'He was guarding the eggs. But they weren't really expecting trouble, or a full paw would have been here.'

'A full paw?'

'Five or six werewolves. Not the full pack, but a full paw.'

'Did you make that up?'

Manners gave a huff of exasperation and ignored the question. 'It doesn't look like anyone else is home. I'm calling it in. We'll move the eggs.'

'And hope Cathill doesn't come back in the meantime.'

'We have daemon-containment charms.'

'Here?'

There was a beat of silence. 'No,' Manners admitted. 'But I'll get back-up to bring some. You can wait in the car if you're feeling antsy.'

I ignored that. 'I'm going to poke about, see if we can find anything else helpful.'

Manners nodded and pulled out his phone, then he swore. 'No signal down here. Stay with the eggs a minute while I go up to call.'

'Sure,' I agreed easily, like I wasn't wholly freaked out to be hanging out in a darkened basement room with a decapitated corpse.

Manners went up the steps, and I looked about for a light switch. We weren't trying to remain concealed any more, and I didn't need to keep wasting my magical energy by running my IR night vision. I found a switch and flipped it, then let the IR fizzle away as light flooded the room.

I'm not very squeamish after all I've seen in my life, but even I swallowed hard at the amount of blood covering me. I tried not to think about it too much. I pulled out my phone and took a picture of the decapitated werewolf.

As I watched, his body started to contort and writhe. I was about to have a small heart attack until I realised that the wolf's body was shifting back to human. When the transition was complete, I took another picture of the body. I walked the short distance to his head and grimaced a little as I turned it over with my toe so I could see his face.

His face was locked in a raging glare that would now be preserved for ever. I took a photo of his face and sent it to Wilf. *Do you know him?* My phone showed no signal so the message would queue until it was ready. Restless and uneasy, I paced the room.

With the shadows chased away, I counted the eggs: twenty-two little fellas. Poor things. What a trauma they'd been through. I didn't know anything about ouroboroses but I felt the need to explain to them. 'Your mum's been looking for you. She's been tearing up the world to find you. You're safe now, though. The dragons and the brethren will take care of you. I expect they know how to deal with eggs.'

I'd always assumed dragons hatched from eggs, but it seemed somewhat ludicrous to imagine a baby Emory crawling out of one. I should probably have a conversation with him about conception, but I didn't want him to take the comments to heart and get hopeful. I was light years away from wanting kids; still, it was something I wanted to know about. Maybe there was an Other library I could track down. There are books on everything.

The silence in the basement was deafening, and the rageful corpse was freaking me out, so I sang lullabies to the eggs. First I cracked out 'Twinkle, Twinkle Little Star', that old classic, then I moved on to 'Peter Rabbit Had a Fly Upon His Nose'. I did the hand gestures and everything. I only felt a little ridiculous, so I think that was a win. Then I heard a creak on the stairs and stopped singing.

Manners descended, looking at me suspiciously. 'I

thought I heard talking.'

I cleared my throat. 'Nope. Is the cavalry en route?'

He nodded.

'Cool. Okay, you secure the eggs, I'll go prowl.' Being nosey is what I do best. It's the bread and butter of any PI, and I have it in spades. Besides, I wanted to get the hell out of Dodge because the werewolf was already starting to smell foul in the confines of the basement.

I searched the kitchen first but all I found were utility bills and take-out menus. Cathill paid the bills promptly and had a liking for Indian food. No red flags there.

The living room was scrupulously tidy and didn't have any clutter: no family photos, no books, nada. It had seats, a fireplace and a huge TV. That was it. Most of the rooms were the same, devoid of any personal or homey touches. It was as warm as a hotel.

Happily, I struck gold in the office. It had a fancy-looking wooden bureau. I tried the drawers but they were locked. I never go anywhere without my handy lock picks so I popped open the leather container and pulled out the torque wrench and the rake.

The lock was really old; all it took was a few rakes and it sprang open. In the bureau were several folders. I pulled one out and started reviewing the contents. It was entitled *Ritual of Shaytan* and filled with glyphs and runes. I found my phone and started taking pictures, but I knew I'd need a witch to translate this. It was fortunate that I had one handy.

I sent a picture of the top page to Lucy and asked if Amber could look at it. I checked the time. It was nearly 10 p.m., so I hoped the girls were still up. I looked at several folders but I had no idea what I was looking at. I kept going until suddenly something in English caught my eye. It was an address.

CHAPTER 28

THE ADDRESS WAS in Caldy, not far from Leo Harfen's residence. A quick Google found that the place had sold about two years ago for a cool £1.5 million. The mansion was an eight-bedroom residence with an outside pool, a driveway complete with Narnia-style lamp posts and an orangery. Whatever that was. We were forty-five minutes away.

I could hear that things were getting busy outside. Several heavy removal vans had rolled up the drive, complete with several brethren teams. I had just finished reading the last folder when my phone sprang to life. It was Wilf. 'Hey,' I said.

'Jinx, you're getting yourself into trouble again.' He sounded affectionate and exasperated.

'It's been a few hours since my last bout of trouble. I was due some more,' I responded lightly.

'The picture you sent is of James Rain, the son of the local alpha, Jimmy Rain.' His tone was sombre.

'Jimmy named his son James?'

'That's what you focus on?' Wilf huffed. 'Jimmy is

bad news, Jinx. I got a lift up here with Lucy, I'm flying under the radar. The council has asked me to investigate Jimmy unofficially. He's the symposium member for the wolves but he's been acting ... erratically. If his son James is there, Jimmy won't be far away. James is a rotten apple that hasn't fallen far from the tree. What have you got yourself involved in?'

I didn't know where to start. 'I don't honestly know. Something to do with the anti-creature movement. There's due to be a big vote in the symposium, and they want to curtail the creatures' freedom. They're using the recent ouroboros' attacks as evidence that some of the creatures go rogue and wreak destruction. They're going to pass a law that all creatures have to be electronically tagged.'

'The creature community won't stand for that,' Wilf said darkly. 'There'll be war.'

'I think that's the objective,' I admitted softly.

'That sounds exactly like something Jimmy would be involved in. You'll need me. Where are you?'

I bit my lip. 'I'm in Liverpool, but I think Jimmy is in Caldy.'

'Tonight is the full moon, Jinx. If something is going down, it'll be today when Jimmy will be at his strongest.'

I swore loudly. That explained why there was only one lonely werewolf guarding Cathill's residence and the eggs. I gave Leo's address to Wilf. 'We'll meet there in an hour,' I suggested. 'We'll just do some recon.'

'You dress for recon, I'll dress for war.' Wilf hung up. Well shit, that had escalated fast.

I called Emory but the phone went straight to voicemail. I left a message. 'Hey, the shit is hitting the fan here. We found the eggs but they were guarded by a werewolf. It's the full moon tonight and Wilf thinks something is going down. I've found another place to check out. I'll take Manners and Wilf with me.' I rattled off the address, just in case. 'I hope things with the trolls are going well. I love you, Emory.' I hung up and tried to ignore the impending sense of doom that suggested I'd been saying a final goodbye.

The door to the office was flung open and Manners burst in. 'Fritz has found another address. It's in the name of Linkage LLP, but it used to belong to Cathill.'

'Let me guess, it's a property in Caldy.'

Manners blinked. 'Yeah.'

I sighed. 'I found reference to it here, too. And I found a load of notes all scrawled in runes. I sent them to Amber. The werewolf downstairs—'

'Is James Rain,' Manners interrupted.

'Yeah. And it's a full moon,' I pointed out.

He rubbed a hand across his face. 'I'll check out the address while you stay here.'

I laughed.

He grimaced. 'It was worth a try.'

'Let's go. And I think we'd better take back-up.'

I followed Manners out of the building. The last of the huge eggs was being carefully boxed up and placed in a removal van.

'That's the last one, sir,' said one of the brethren, quivering to attention but managing not to snap out a salute. Ex-military, I guessed. Like the rest of the brethren, he was musclebound, with a strong frame and a readiness about him that suggested he was always ready to fight. He had pale skin dusted with freckles; he looked young but his eyes told a different story. He'd seen or done dark things.

Manners nodded. 'Good work, Alfie, but we're not done yet. Half of you take the eggs to the caves and secure them. The rest of you are with me. The night is young.'

I was dying to ask more about the caves, but I held my silence. Half of the men swung into the removal vans and the rest climbed into black Range Rover Evoques. They must be the brethren's company cars. I gave them Leo Harfen's address and we moved out.

Alfie and a chap called Graham joined Manners and me in the car. Graham gave me a friendly nod. I'd just fastened my seatbelt when my phone rang again. My heart leapt, thinking it was Emory; I tried not to be disappointed that it was Lucy. 'Hey, Luce, did you get those pictures I sent?' I asked.

'Yeah. You've turned Amber into a crazy person.

233

She's scrawling down translations and muttering to herself. But the headline? It's a ritual to summon daemons.'

I sighed. 'Of course it is.'

'The ritual needs to be done under the light of the full moon.' She paused. 'That's tonight.'

'Yeah.'

'So where do you need us?' Lucy asked.

I needed her far away, safe with Gato. However, I needed Amber. And if we were tangling with a werewolf pack, Wilf would need support too – and Lucy and Gato were it. I gave her Leo's address with dread curling in my tummy.

'I'll drive while Amber carries on translating,' Lucy said. 'We'll be there in thirty minutes.' She rang off.

I turned to Manners. 'The documents I found are rituals to summon daemons during a full moon.'

Manners nodded calmly. 'We've got daemon-containment charms with us.'

I thought of the battle of the Bombed-Out Church, which felt a lifetime ago. 'We had those last time we tangled with Cathill, and he still got away.'

'Then the witch that made them wasn't to be trusted. Amber did these.' That was something. Not much, but something.

I touched Glimmer in my pocket. Its weight felt reassuring. I wasn't a soldier, a fighter, but with Glimmer I didn't need to be. It was a weapon, and it made me into one too. I rang Leo to let him know that a small crowd was on its way. I got his voicemail, but it would have to do.

I needed all the help I could get. I debated before sending off a few more text messages, summons for help that I didn't want to make. I didn't want any of my friends to die because they were coming to my aid, but my gut said I'd need more than Manners and his team to face what was coming.

CHAPTER 29

WHEN WE ARRIVED at Leo's residence, the atmosphere was grim. Lucy and Wilf were talking quietly, and Amber was still hunched over her phone, scribbling away translations. Leo was leaning on a staff, and he had a sword strapped to his hip. There were half a dozen other elves dressed similarly, including Leo's daughter, Erin.

'You can't be serious.' I pointed at Leo's sword. 'You're ancient.'

Leo cackled. 'You're as old as you feel, my dear. And I feel young.'

'You're going to feel dead,' I argued.

'If it is my time. My time? Get it?' He laughed. Leo's grasp on reality had been tenuous before; now it seemed shot to hell.

'Save yourself the bother, *inspector*,' Erin said to me, laying sarcastic emphasis on the title. When I'd first met her, I'd flashed Stone's ID and pretended to be an inspector.

I winced. 'Sorry about that,' I muttered.

'Indeed. Well, I've been arguing with my father about this for weeks but he won't be dissuaded. Apparently the elves are going to fight the daemons.'

'Daemons? Plural?'

Leo nodded, beaming. He was slightly deranged – too much time in the Third realm. 'Oh yes. Lots of daemons. Sky is quite mad.' He was one to talk.

I resisted the urge to scream. The elves had known about the daemon ritual and said nothing about it to anyone. This society was so fractured it made a broken mirror look flawless.

'We'd better get going,' Leo said. 'It's starting now.'

I checked the time: 11:10 p.m. 'It's not midnight yet!'

'Who said anything about midnight?' Leo asked dreamily. 'The time is now, or as now as any time can ever be. This way. We'll go on foot.' The doddering old elf took off with sure footsteps, literally leading us down the garden path.

Manners and his men had been ignoring the conversation as they strapped on bullet-proof vests and armed themselves with guns and knives. There were dressed in black, their faces marked with camouflage paint. They followed the elves silently.

'Amber,' I called. 'We've got to move.'

She stood muttering, frowning at the screen. 'That can't be right.'

Wilf tucked a hand under her arm and started pulling

her gently along the path. Lucy, Gato and I brought up the rear. Gato was in full battle-cat mode with black obsidian spikes and red eyes. He – and my parents – were ready to wreak havoc.

'Sorry I pulled you all into this,' I sighed. 'I'd rather you were all home safe.'

Lucy touched Gato. 'Your mum says there's nowhere they would rather be than by your side. Besides, Isaac is happy to be in battle mode. He's ready for a rampage. He says it's been too long.' She shrugged. 'Well, I think that's what he says. His thoughts aren't as clear as your parents, they're more flashes of feelings and images. I'll get better at this piping thing. Your dad says to be careful.'

I smiled. 'I'm always careful.'

Lucy snorted. 'Sure. As careful as a bull in a china shop.'

'If the bull was considerate, he'd be super-careful,' I pointed out.

Lucy gave me a flat look and I winked. I was trying to keep up the banter but my knees were knocking. Cathill was only one daemon, but he'd helped to kidnap Nate and Hes, poisoned Emory's adopted parents and been a terrifying force at the Battle of the Bombed-Out church. What would a *crowd* of daemons be capable of? We needed to shut this down before the ritual was completed. We didn't need more of them floating around the Other realm.

The line in front of us halted, and we started to spread out. I recognised the property from the Zoopla pictures that I'd Googled. We were at the bottom of the lawn, but we were on the wrong side of the hedge.

Lucy and Wilf started to remove their clothes in preparation for their shift, and I averted my eyes.

Manners moved silently to my side. 'As far as we can see, there's a full pack down there but some of them are in cages.'

'Why would they be in cages?' I asked, confused.

Amber spoke up suddenly. 'Hosts for all of the daemons they intend to summon.'

Manners grimaced. 'We don't have enough containment charms for that many daemons. We need to stop this now.'

'You're preaching to the choir,' Amber muttered. 'Let me get closer so I can see what we're dealing with.'

Manners led Amber, Gato and I to a spot in the hedge where it wasn't so thick so we could peer through. Amber squinted into the darkness and swore. I looked over her shoulder so I could see what was making her so angry.

Stone and Ajay were there, next to Sky. Stone was gesturing wildly, looking furious, but Ajay was watching the scene coolly and giving nothing away. Sky was ignoring Stone. She was flanked by the two hulking bodyguards Emory and I had met in her office. They were watching Stone with open hostility.

Maybe Stone had had a change of heart. Whatever his beef was with the creature community, summoning a shedload of daemons was not going to help the situation.

I scanned the lawn. Sure enough, there were cages around the pool, five down each of the long sides and one at each end. Twelve daemons. With Cathill, that would make a total of thirteen. A tingle ran down my spine. That would be bad.

'She's not just summoning a few daemons,' Amber ground out. 'She's opening a portal.'

'Can you tell where to?'

'To the daemon dimension.'

I pinched my nose. 'There's a daemon dimension?' Amber nodded. 'What am I going to get tattooed on my head now? A Rubik cube?'

She ignored my facetious comment. Our attention was drawn back to the garden as the shouting increased. A Connection detective came forwards, pulling a young woman behind him. Her hands were bound and she was sobbing helplessly.

'Amelia Jane!' Amber gasped, leaning forwards as if she were about to leap though the hedge.

Manners caught her and held her back. 'We need a plan,' he growled.

Sky smirked at Amelia Jane but across the distance we couldn't make out her words. Then she removed a dagger from a sheath on her hip and, without a change in her expression, reached out and slit Amelia Jane's throat. Then Sky tossed her bleeding corpse into the pool.

As Amelia Jane's blood struck the water, the pool lit up with flames as if her body was made of potassium. Sparks flew and the pool bubbled and frothed as it set itself on fire. It blazed, an inferno dancing on top of the water.

Stone shouted incoherently in rage and drew his lighter, flicked it and summoned his blade of flames. He lunged towards Sky and her bodyguards moved in to defend her. She ignored it all; she was still muttering, gesturing at the pool.

'Amelia! My God, Amelia. I'm so sorry. We're too late,' Amber whispered mournfully, a tear ghosting down her face. 'Sky's opened the portal. God damn it – what is she thinking?' She shook herself and dashed angrily at the solitary tear. 'We need to close the portal before she seals it open.'

'How do we close it?'

'We need a sacrifice.'

I bit my lip. 'Like we all agree to give up chocolate?'

Amber gave me a dark look full of scorn; she wasn't into jokes just now. 'Like one of us agrees to give up our life.'

'Fuck. Rock-Paper-Scissors?'

'I'm the oldest. Jake is dead and Amelia is dead. I'll paint the closing runes and then I'll step through.' She seemed determined, and we didn't have time to waste.

To be honest, I didn't want to volunteer to die. I was twenty-five and I hadn't been married, or snorkelling on the Great Barrier Reef, or bareback horse riding. I wasn't enamoured of the idea of dying, not with so much to live for. Not without one last kiss. How was I to know that my last kiss with Emory had been my *last kiss* with Emory? No, I didn't want to die today. But I didn't want Amber to die, either. She'd grown on me, the stubborn old boot.

'That's plan B,' I said firmly.

'What's plan A?' Amber asked drily.

'Plan A is none of us dying.'

'And we're going to accomplish that how?' Manners asked.

'I'm still working on that part,' I admitted.

Amber shook her head. 'Whatever our plan is, we need to get me to the poolside so I can paint the closing runes around it. And we need to move *now*.'

Manners turned to me. 'Can you blast a hole in this hedge?'

I summoned my intention. 'Now?'

'Now!' Amber said urgently.

'Ready,' Manners said to his men. They all clicked off the safety catches on their guns. With them having no magic, it felt like they were bringing knives to a gun fight. I felt responsible for them being there, and I prayed that we'd make it out of it alive.

I needed a hole in the hedge, a giant hole, so we could all get through at once. 'Hole!' I ordered, pushing out my intention. Suddenly half the hedge disappeared and we were standing behind nothing. Oops: I hadn't meant for the hole to be quite so big. I really sucked at the IR.

The wolves meandering around the pool spotted us instantly and let out howls of alarm. Then the uncaged wolves started racing towards us.

CHAPTER 30

I TRIED TO count the ravening wolves but they were moving too quickly. There were fifty at least, maybe sixty. Too many. Way too many. But we had no choice, we had to stop Sky and close the portal.

I hoped some of my text messages had been picked up. Why hadn't I just called? Maybe I'd wanted to leave it to fate – dammit, what an idiot thought. We made our own destinies, and right now mine was looking bleak.

I wished I had Nate with me. I'd feel better if he was here to wade into this mess with me. He'd had my back time and time again, but I guessed that in the end he couldn't get over his dragon–brethren prejudices, and he wasn't willing to fight on the side of the creatures. I tried not to feel disappointed because I'd thought that he and Emory had made some significant progress.

I missed Nate and I missed Emory. Hell, I wished I had some more allies. Even the murderous Bastion would be a welcome addition to Team Suicide Mission.

As if I had summoned him with my thoughts, I saw a shape move against the night sky, blocking out the stars with its body and its huge wingspan. It let out a fierce shriek, momentarily distracting the hordes of wolves from their forward motion. They pulled together cautiously, eyes on the sky, looking at the predator above them. I couldn't tell from that distance if it was Bastion or Shirdal, but either way with a griffin above us our odds of survival had just improved. Maybe only fractionally, but any improvement was a plus.

'Go! While they're distracted!' Manners shouted to the brethren.

We ran towards the wolves and unleashed mayhem. Guns roared and the wolves howled. Wilf and Lucy were in their wolf forms, and they ran together towards the wolf pack. Lucy's fur was white and grey, while Wilf's was black and gold; it would be hard to distinguish them in the dark when they mixed with the rival pack. They ran in tandem and attacked as a unit, moving together in a way that shouldn't have been possible for two wolves who barely knew each other. I wondered if Lucy had piped Wilf's wolf.

Wilf and Lucy reached their opponents and started rending flesh with tooth and claw. Howls of pain filled the air as bullets and teeth ripped into the wolf pack. The brethren were fighting in teams, trying in vain to keep the wolves from tearing into them. Human and wolf blood sprayed the field.

I saw Cathill smirking from the shadows, watching

the destruction with open glee. He was dressed in jeans and a casual shirt; he looked a little like Heath Ledger, but with longer surfer-dude hair. He had three triangles on his head and a circle around them. As with all vampyrs, he was seriously good looking. And he wasn't alone.

'Vampyres!' I shouted a warning. They weren't Volderiss vamps, more's the pity.

A light flared near Cathill, and I watched as he summoned and flung a ball of flame towards the brethren units below. I summoned water and poured it, sprayed it towards the careening fireball until all that was left were sparks and embers.

Cathill let out a roar of rage that twisted his handsome face. Something otherworldly crept over him, and a shudder ran down my spine. The daemon was awake, and he was looking right at me. I'd pissed him off. Fuck.

'Good job,' Leo said from behind me. 'Keep him distracted.'

Before I could respond, Leo and Erin were darting to the shadows and heading towards Cathill. I hoped they had containment charms.

'Morris!' I heard Manners holler. 'Come here, you bloody bastard!'

I didn't have time to worry about Manners facing off with Cathill's second-in-command. Manners was strong and competent, but he was human and mortal; Morris was neither of those things. Even so, I had to focus on

Cathill or Cathill would kill me.

I stood like a human water fountain, spraying endless streams of water towards the flames Cathill kept throwing towards me. Once again the fire and water combination was creating fog, but this time we were in the open air, and the fog was crawling along the ground like a blanket. Luckily it wasn't rising too high so we could all see, though it was making it harder for the wolves who were standing lower down.

I had a moment of anxiety as I looked again for Lucy's lighter coat. Cathill took advantage of my distraction to send a hot ball of flame right at me. Gato leapt into me, pushing me to the ground. He growled a little at me, and I accepted the telling off; now was not the time to go wool-gathering.

Gato gave me a lick and bounded off. Their body, complete with obsidian spikes, slammed into the next unfortunate werewolf who crossed their path. I kept low, under the cover of the fog.

'Jiiiiiiiiiiinx,' Cathill called tauntingly. 'Come out, come out, wherever you are!' He said it in a sing-song voice. And then I felt it: a pressure on my mind, a need to obey him, to jump up and show him where I was. Mind control.

I shuddered against the pressure. My head felt like it was splitting in two, and my thoughts slowed and crawled. I was half way to standing before my hand brushed against Glimmer in my pocket. It sang its own song into my mind and chased away the daemon's compulsion. Glimmer's song was scornful, and it chastised me; I wasn't Cathill's creature, I was Glimmer's.

I let out a breath of relief as the iron grip on my mind eased and disappeared. Thank goodness Glimmer was with me or I would have been a marionette in Cathill's deadly puppet show.

'Come on Jinx, come and play,' Cathill ordered more sharply, annoyance colouring his tone as I ignored his compulsion.

I crawled closer to him then suddenly remembered that stealth wasn't the object of the game. I was supposed to be distracting him from Leo and Erin. I stood up, showing myself to Cathill, and he beamed approvingly. 'Ah, there you are, Jinx! I'm so glad you've come out to play!'

While I'd been hiding in the fog, he'd been building a fireball bigger than any other he'd thrown. I didn't know if I could stop it but I had no option; I had to try. I was scared but adrenaline was pumping through me and distracting me from my fear. If I wanted to emerge from this still breathing, I needed to fight. And I really wanted to come out of this swinging.

Cathill's fire bowled towards me, and I summoned my own flame. Reaching out, I encircled his flameball with my own sheet of fire as if I were wrapping a present.

248

When it was fully encircled and I tried to control it, it was like wrestling with a heavy, lumbering bear. Sweat broke out on my forehead as I pushed the malignant sphere of flames towards the pool, the nearest body of water that could extinguish it.

Cathill's smirk turned to a frown. 'Now that's not playing nicely, Jinx,' he chastised. 'I thought we were friends.' *Lie.*

He held out his hands to build another fireball, and I wondered how long I could keep this up. All around me were the sounds of battle. There were shots and grunts and groans. Someone was crying. Wearily I prepared myself to face what was coming – but nothing else came.

Cathill's frown turned into apoplectic rage. 'What have you done?' he screamed. 'What have you done?'

Erin stepped out of the shadows holding an old-fashioned lamp in her hands. 'Containment charm,' she said calmly. 'Bye-bye.'

Cathill screamed and three carefully placed crystals around him started to glow. His body swayed and he crumbled into dust and bone. A black shadow with horns and a gaping mouth of razor-sharp teeth spun into the lamp.

I sagged in relief. 'So now he's a freaking genie?'

'Something like that,' Erin agreed. 'We'll lock him up. The elves guard the daemons that wander into the Other realm. If we hadn't let the Connection admit him the first time, all of this could have been prevented. Now we need to close the portal.'

She was right. I'd let Cathill distract me but we still needed to stop Sky and close the portal. Cathill was one daemon; we couldn't let any more come across into the Other realm.

As if I'd summoned it with my thoughts, the blazing inferno in the pool suddenly darkened and a shadow slipped out, a shadow with burning eyes and horns. Fuck. It flew effortlessly towards the werewolves imprisoned in the cages. The wolf nearest started to howl in distress. The noise started out as a high-pitched bark and quickly turned into a piercing scream, a warning to the others.

The howl cut off abruptly as the daemon sank into the werewolf. The werewolf shook itself once, and when it opened its eyes, they were glowing red. Great. Just what we needed.

I ran forwards, towards Sky. Alfie was in hand-to-hand combat with one of her bodyguards. One of the other bodyguards was already dead, but this one was a seasoned detective and a wizard. One moment Alfie was standing there, the next moment his body exploded like he'd had a grenade planted inside of him. The brethren were like lambs to the slaughter; they didn't stand a chance against these bastards. And I'd brought them here.

The murderous bodyguard grinned. 'It's raining brethren.'

Fury swept through me. Two could play at that game. I summoned a fireball and sent it flying towards him at speed. It struck him in the chest and knocked him off his feet. His skin sizzled and burned. I ignored his screams and turned to Sky. 'Why are you doing this?' I demanded. 'The daemons won't help you. They have their own agenda.'

'And I have mine. With thirteen daemons in the Other realm, the Verdict will come tumbling down. Their magic is too much to contain. And then the walls between the realms come down – no more darting back and forth, dependant on the portals to recharge. The Common realm will know us, and the Connection can rule supreme.'

I stared at her. 'You're mad. The Common realm isn't ready for us. They'll bomb us with nukes before they bow down to some superior magical power.'

She shrugged. 'They can try. We'll re-direct their missiles to creature populations. It would be quite helpful really.'

'You're crazy!' Stone interjected. 'Sky, this is madness. Close the portal!'

She sighed. 'Young Zachary, you were such a disappointment to your father. He had so many plans for you but you just wanted to play inspector. Well, be a good inspector and do what the symposium member tells you. This is for the good of all.' Sky pointed to me. 'Now kill her.'

Stone lifted his fiery sword but, instead of attacking me, he dived towards Sky. He decapitated her with one effortlessly smooth motion. It was Stone's signature move but she wasn't expecting it. Her eyes were wide and shocked as her head rolled off her shoulders and plopped into the pool's fiery water.

Ajay shrieked, 'Zach! How could you?' He reached for the sword on his hip, drew it from its scabbard and held it defiantly. He murmured a word and flames danced along the metal. Amber darted forwards behind him, her ever-present black tote bag over her shoulder. She pulled out her jars and paintbrushes and started to paint runes on the poolside slabs.

Stone saw what she was doing. He let his eyes slide away from her and danced back, drawing Ajay's attention. 'Ajay,' he said pleadingly, 'don't do this. I don't want to fight you. You're like a brother to me – you always have been.' Stone let his flame sword extinguish.

'Brother or not, you choose Jinx over us, over the cause!' Ajay screamed.

'This isn't anti-creature – this is anti-magic. Breaking the Verdict is madness. The realms work because they're separate. Sky was crazy.'

'Sky was a genius! She was my mentor! She's guided me for years. She took me under her wing when no one else would touch me. She didn't care that I'd worked with Faltease. Back then, I didn't understand how perverted his aims were, that our magic was an inherited gift. Turning people Other was wrong. But Sky taught me, she taught me everything. And I've spent years undoing my mistakes, just as she bade me.'

'It was you,' I hissed in realisation. 'You killed The Twenty!'

'Seventeen,' Ajay growled. 'That bloody griffin killed three of them for me. It's not right. They were mine to end because I'd helped to create them. It was my duty.'

He didn't know my parents were alive, and that was one small mercy. Bastion killing their bodies really had protected them and their secret, but now their maker and hunter stood before me. Ajay was the reason they had run and hidden and lived in secret for eighteen long years.

I drew Glimmer again. 'Fuck you, Ajay!'

He grinned at me, maniacal and twisted, so unlike the friendly warm man I thought I'd known. Then he leapt towards me.

I raised Glimmer but Stone pushed me back, ready to fight in my place. He drew his own blade and met Ajay's sword with it. The air rang with the sound of steel. Ajay's flames danced down Stone's sword but a whispered word from Stone extinguished them.

'I've always been better than you,' Ajay taunted. 'Your father taught me to fight. I've always been your father's man.'

Ajay had once said that he'd always been Stone's

man, and I'd assumed he meant Zach's, but he'd meant *Gilligan*'s. He'd been Lord Stone's man all along. When would I learn that just because something pinged *true* it didn't always make it so? People were master wordsmiths and liars; omission and half-truths still misled me when I wasn't careful.

'Your father recruited me before Faltease came along. Your dad taught me to worm my way into the dragons.' Ajay laughed. 'And talking of worms, here she comes!' *True.* The ground trembled and the vibrations shuddered through my feet.

As Stone looked over his shoulder towards the lawn, Ajay lurched forwards and sliced deeply into his body. Stone let out a low groan as blood bubbled out of the wound.

'I told you I was better than you,' Ajay shouted. 'All these years I've had to pretend that you were superior to me. I used to piss you off a little, just a blatant use of the Third realm now and again, because I could.'

I remembered that the first time I'd met Ajay he'd disappeared faster than I could see. He'd used the Third to slow time so he could run faster. Little signs were there even then, if we'd known to look.

Stone shook his head. 'I love you like a brother. Don't make me kill you. Put your sword down.' *True.* There was anguish in Stone's voice as he pleaded with Ajay; his desperation was palpable.

I could feel the building vibrating through the patio slabs. Ajay was right, the ouroboros was coming – and she wasn't the only one. More black shadows were slipping out of the portal and sliding into the unwilling wolves that were waiting in cages.

The possessed wolves started to throw themselves rhythmically against the cage doors. Amber risked a shout to me. 'Use your empathy to calm them down!' she ordered. 'You can't control the daemons, so try to influence the wolves!'

'How the hell do I do that?' I yelled back.

'How do I know? I'm not a bloody empath. You need to *project!*'

Amber's shouting had drawn Ajay's attention, and he swore viciously as he saw what she was doing on the slabs. 'Oh no, you don't. You're not sabotaging Sky's final work.' His face was dark, his lips curling back in rage. He stalked towards Amber, sword raised.

Stone was far closer than I was. 'Help her! Help Amber!' I begged Stone.

He nodded and pushed himself up, blood dripping with every step. 'I'm not done with you yet, Ajay, not by a long way,' he taunted. 'You got in a lucky strike but you won't do it again.'

Ajay took the bait and turned back to Stone. Amber continued to paint frantically. I shut off the sounds of the fighting around me and turned my attention to the cages.

Ten of the wolves were now hammering against the doors; they'd soon be through them. Elves were placing crystals and muttering on either side of three of the cages, but that still left seven daemons ready to wreak havoc on the Other realm.

I closed my eyes and practised my dad's breathing exercises, but they didn't work. I had nothing – and no idea what to do next. My concentration was shot to shit as the ground exploded.

I opened my eyes just in time to see mud spraying everywhere as the ouroboros made her entrance. This time her eyes weren't shrouded in rage. She was on our side – she just needed to know it.

CHAPTER 31

L UCY MADE THE same connection. She transformed back into human form and, naked and weary, staggered towards the ouroboros. Lucy looked like she'd been crying, and my heart went out to her. I prayed she was okay and that she was telling the mama ouroboros that we'd found and secured her eggs. I think the message must have got across because the ouroboros dived back into the rival wolf pack, using its killer teeth to chomp the wolves in two.

I searched anxiously for Wilf among the wolves then my stomach dropped and tears filled my eyes. Wilf was next to Lucy; he was back in human form, and his body was covered in dozens of cuts, the deepest of which was a ragged slice across his throat. He was unnaturally still and had the pallor of death. Now I knew the source of Lucy's tears. Gato stood next to Wilf's corpse and let out a mournful howl. It echoed and for a moment all was still.

I was frozen, stuck in a hellish moment of loss. Wilf had taken so long to bury his way into my heart but now he was there forever. He'd cared for me for years, had tried everything he could think of to force me into the realm I should have been born into. I was who I was because of him and his machinations. And now he was gone. Tears streamed unchecked down my cheeks.

A steady metal thudding drew me back. 'Jinx!' Amber screamed. 'Do something! I need another minute at least.'

Stone and Ajay were still fighting. Stone was keeping Ajay from Amber, letting her finish the runes. The caged wolves were thundering against the metal doors. The cages were heavy and solid, designed to withstand a werewolf breaking out of them, but the wolves were amped up with daemon juice, and the doors were bowing. It wouldn't be long before they shattered. And their eyes were locked on Amber.

Fuck. If they got free, they were going straight for her, and then nothing would close the portal.

'Jess!' Lucy shouted, her hand on Gato's broad shoulder. 'Your mum says let the ocean recede and imagine it snowing on the beach. Imagine the snow being calm. Project calm into the snow and let the snow settle everywhere.'

My mind was in chaos, and I was grateful to have an order to follow. I closed my eyes and did as she'd said. I let the sounds of the ocean recede but it was too much; I was overwhelmed with anger and malevolence and pain and fear. I gasped at the tide of it all, awash and lost.

But then love came, steady and strong. Louder than

anger, louder than fear, it thrummed through me. I opened my eyes to meet Gato's, and I smiled at my parents. I hooked my arms around Gato's neck, spikes and all, and I tried again. This time I let the love surround me and lift me up, then I summoned calm. I breathed as my dad had shown me so many times.

With their love steadying me, I let it snow in my mindscape. I pictured the snow settling around me, and when it lay in a thick blanket, I opened my eyes. I was projecting calm around me as far as I could. The caged werewolves had stopped throwing themselves against the metal enfolding them; some were even lying down with their heads resting on their paws.

The calm hadn't simply spread to the wolves but to Amber, who was finishing her rune work clear-eyed, and to Ajay who turned back to Stone with no more rage in his eyes. A deathly intent remained, however. 'Let's finish this,' he said evenly. He raised his sword again, and his weariness was obvious.

Exhaustion was in Stone's every movement, and the wound to his torso was deep and bleeding freely. A lesser man would have been on his knees, but Stone always had the strength and determination to do what was right. His definition of right and wrong might have varied from mine from time to time, but for now we were on the same page.

Stone needed help. I gathered my intention and

summoned fire from within. With regret, I built a flame that would *burn* and held it in my hands, its heat crackling my skin. I waited until the right moment, and then I flung it at Ajay. It wasn't heroic, and it wasn't nice. The flames struck Ajay's back, and he cried out and whirled to face me. In doing so he left himself exposed to Stone.

Stone raised his sword. He met my eyes as he sliced through Ajay's neck, decapitating one of his dearest friends. Now that the ocean had receded, I felt the grief and regret that were already pulling at him, but he didn't let it stop him from doing what he needed to do.

As Ajay's lifeless body slid to the ground, so did Stone. He buckled at the knees, his sword dropping from his numb fingers. His wounds from fighting Ajay were numerous and deep. Stone was dying. I had no healing skills, no healing spittle, I had nothing with which to save him.

My agony was written on my face, but Stone smiled even as he struggled to breathe. 'I'm still so grateful to have met you, Jessica Sharp, even if you were my own jinx in the end. I have loved you as much as I could anyone.' *True.* That it was true drew tears to my eyes. He honestly loved me. I felt wretched.

'Stone... Zach...' Even now, as he lay dying, I couldn't say the words back to him. He'd latched onto me, the first person to see him as a man and not just as an inspector and bogeyman. I hadn't exactly showered him with affection, but I doubted he'd had much from Gilligan as a child. In some ways, it wasn't surprising that he'd felt so strongly for me; we'd been through a crucible of fire together, a magical few days that I couldn't regret, even now I knew what would follow.

Stone's smile turned sorrowful. 'One day you might have loved me if I hadn't compelled you. I'm sorry for that. I regret it more than you can know.' *True.*

I could give him that much. 'Yes, I might have – one day,' I admitted softly, and I wasn't surprised when it rang true.

'I'm sorry about the spider.' Stone coughed. 'But I'm not sorry about the damned Mercedes. Bloody dragon, buying your love.'

'It was you? All of the attempts on my life were masterminded by you?'

He smiled ruefully. 'I was just trying to distract the Prime from tomorrow's vote. Nothing personal and none of the attacks were serious, I made sure my orders were clear on that. No one was to actually harm you. I knew Gato would spot the spider and you'd find your balance from a little shove and the car wouldn't actually run you over. I made sure the firebomb was only used when you were out of the car. I wouldn't let them really hurt you, Jinx, I swear to you. I just needed to distract that damned dragon.'

Stone coughed again and this time dark blood splattered onto his hands. He grimaced and flicked his eyes to Amber, who was still busy painting runes. She could save his life – if she went to him quickly.

I opened my mouth to call her over, then closed it again with a clack. The portal needed to be closed and she couldn't be interrupted until she was done. I cleared my throat and tried to distract Stone from his pain. It was all I could do. 'You wanted to distract Emory from the vote to tag all the creatures – to mark them like Hitler marked the Jews. How could you think that was right?'

Stone sighed. 'I don't. Grief makes you do stupid things. I was raised anti-creature. Father spewed that crap at me my whole life, but I was determined to be a fair inspector, and gradually I saw that he was wrong. All of us are dangerous in our own ways, both creature and human. Sky is proof of that. But I needed to get my father's approval, to finish his work, to honour his memory. For all his faults, he was my father. I loved him, and I never stopped wanting him to love me. For what it's worth, I regret my whole involvement in this mess. I was arguing with Sky and threatening to pull my support from her in the vote when you arrived.'

'Done!' Amber called out triumphantly. She stood up, dropped her paintbrush and stared at the flames still burning on the pool – the open portal that she intended to step through to end it all. A sacrifice was still needed, and I still didn't have a Plan A.

Amber took a deep breath but Gato was already rushing forwards. They leapt into the portal together, into the fire, and I screamed and screamed and screamed. Gato floated, suspended by the water and the flames.

'Mum! Dad!' I sobbed. I strode towards the pool's edge, intent on getting them back. The flames were already dying down, and the portal was closing. Their sacrifice had been accepted.

I was bending to dive in when strong arms pulled me back. Stone. 'No, Jinx, you can't.'

'They're my parents!' I explained desperately, struggling against his arms. How could he still be so strong when he was dying just as Gato was?

'What?' he asked in confusion.

'My parents, they're in my hound. They transferred their consciousness. I won't let them die. What would *you* do to bring back your father? Let me go! I can't lose them again.' I was in agony.

Another presence nudged urgently against my mind. Emory. I looked up and his giant form plummeted down across the moon. Stone looked up and saw him. His arms were already weakening around me, and I renewed my struggle. 'Sorry, Jinx,' he murmured. 'I can't risk you. But I'm dying, and maybe the gods will be kind.'

He took a deep breath and summoned the last of his energy. 'Bind,' he murmured. Ropes from around one of the cages leapt up and wrapped around me as I screamed in frustration.

Stone looked up at Emory. 'Get Gato out of the portal!' he roared at the sky.

Emory plummeted. At the last moment, he beat his massive scarlet wings above the pool and his mammoth claws reached down and curled carefully around my soaking wet hound. As Emory lifted back and pulled Gato from the water, Stone dived in. He cried out as his blood swirled in the pool and met the remainder of the flames. They flared around his body, and in a blink, he disappeared and so did the daemonic flames.

The portal was finally closed and Stone ... Stone was gone.

CHAPTER 32

WITH THE CLOSURE of the portal, the remainder of the werewolf pack that had survived the ravages of the ouroboros, and the griffin drew together and ran for the hole in the hedge. The brethren, battered and bleeding, let them go. Cathill's vampyrs slid back into the shadows and phased away. All that was left of our enemies were the dead – and the daemons.

Amber had wasted no time and was frantically painting containment runes on the remaining cages that didn't have crystals glowing around them. It was a temporary measure; more containment charms would be needed to secure the daemons completely, but it would do for now. The elves were doing their thing, chanting and holding out lamps to imprison the daemons. One by one the cages were emptying; the werewolf hosts had to be sacrificed to secure the daemons. More elves had joined the others so they had six sets of crystals now, but that still left four unbound daemons.

My mind was blank as I stared at the unmoving body of my stupid, wonderful, self-sacrificing hell hound. Then one of Emory's massive feet carefully pushed against Gato's chest, once, twice, three times. At the third push, Gato's chest rose of its own volition and he sat up weakly, coughing up water.

I started to sob in relief and barely registered Emory's claws slicing carefully through the ropes that bound me. All I knew was that I could move again. I threw myself down next to my beloved hound, my parents. 'Are you okay?' I asked desperately, searching Gato's eyes. 'Are you all okay?' Gato hung his head and my heart stopped. 'Lucy!' I screamed, 'Lucy! I need you.'

She came with haunted eyes, naked, battered and bruised. She reached out and touched Gato's head then she met my eyes and shook her head helplessly.

'Tell me,' I managed to say.

'To close the portal... Your mum went first... I'm sorry. Your mum's gone. I'm sorry, Jinx.'

'Is Dad okay? Isaac?' I choked out.

'They're still here,' she whispered.

I nodded. 'Okay.' I swallowed hard. For so long the fact that my parents were dead had defined me as much as my eye colour or my job. That I'd had Mum back briefly was a twist of fate that was equally cruel and kind. We'd had more time together but it was still not enough. It never would be.

Grief settled over me like a well-worn cloak. It fitted me well, as it had for a long time. The loss of my mother was complex but it wasn't sharp and new. She'd been gone for so long; having her back was but a blip of joy, here and gone in a heartbeat. I knew grief well, and I let it enter my heart like an old friend. My mum was gone forever.

Emory had changed back to his human form, complete with an immaculate suit that was so at odds with the scene around us. He pulled me to him tightly, tucking me under his chin. His left arm was wrapped around my shoulders, and his other hand ran steadily up and down my back, soothing me.

I could feel his own loss at my mum's death, his concern for me and, through it all, his love. It steadied me at the edge of the abyss and let me breathe. Perhaps someday soon I would wail and gnash my teeth, but not now. I couldn't break now. The day wasn't done. We still had so much to do, and I was weary, bone tired of it all, and tired of being the one that lost.

I took a deep breath and returned Emory's hug. Finally, I gave him a squeeze and stepped away from his arms to kneel next to Gato. I wrapped my arms around my soaking dog, not caring about the water that soaked me in turn.

'I'm sorry, Dad,' I whispered, giving Gato a kiss on the muzzle. I'd lost Mum long ago, but this was the first time *he'd* lost her, and I could read the abject misery in Gato's –*Dad's* – eyes. I gave him one last kiss. 'I've got to check on the others,' I murmured.

My mum wasn't the only loss. Gato lay down, shifting from Battle Cat to loveable Great Dane. He curled in on himself and let out a low whimper. I gave him one last stroke and stood up. I couldn't make this better. They needed to wrap their heads and hearts around the fact that Mum was gone, and I needed to do something, *anything*.

Lucy let out a low groan. As she swayed on her feet, Emory leapt forwards to catch her. The triangle rune disappeared from her forehead, and she fainted as the Other kicked her out. Emory laid her down carefully on the patio, shrugged out of his suit jacket and covered her with it, somewhat belatedly protecting her modesty.

I checked Lucy was alright, but she was out for the count. I needed to do something to help. I started moving down the lawn where the dead and injured were strewn. Amber was already wading in, paintbrush and magical gloop at the ready. She was snapping gloves on and off as she frantically painted healing runes, triaging the patients by eye and proximity.

Emory was walking among his men, closing the eyes of the fallen, murmuring words of reassurance and thanks to the injured.

'DeLea – over here!' Tom cried. He was in the shadows at the edge of the lawn, and a body lay in front of him.

I saw a flash of pink in the darkness and dread curled in my stomach. Amber, Emory and I ran over. It was Manners; he was unconscious but his wounds were open and gaping.

Amber shook her head regretfully. 'I'm sorry. His wounds are too severe – they're beyond my ability to heal. He's out, he's not in pain. I'm sorry,' she repeated. She turned and headed back to the ones that she could save.

I stared down at Manners and shook my head. I couldn't face losing him – I'd even let him call me Toots again. Inspiration struck and I fumbled in my pocket. My fingers closed around the cool metal of Glimmer, and it sang once more, crooning and triumphant. It had saved me from the crushing grip of Cathill, and now I prayed it could save Manners.

I swallowed hard and hoped I wouldn't see this moment in my nightmares. Manners was all kinds of torn up; the vampyr he'd fought had used fangs and blade against him. Righteous anger only gets you so far, and Manners hadn't stood a chance. His chest rose and fell with a sticky, sucking sound that felt like it wasn't far off a death rattle.

I'd used Glimmer once before, and once again I needed a miracle. 'Make him a wolf,' I whispered. 'Save him.' Werewolves could heal huge amounts of damage, as could vampyrs, but I didn't have a friendly vamp to hand

269

so I had no choice.

I pushed Nate out of my mind and focused on Manners. Faltease had been nuts, but it was do or die. With a sharp breath, I raised Glimmer and stabbed Manners in the heart. I eased the blade out and watched, feeling sick as Manners' blood soaked into Glimmer and disappeared. I held my breath and waited.

'He's healing!' Tom gasped with relief.

We all watched as Manners' skin started to knit together. 'I think he's going to make it,' I breathed. Thank goodness I'd stabbed the werewolf, James Rain.

I turned into Emory's arms once more and hugged him tighter. I couldn't have taken one more loss, but Manners was going to be okay. He'd really grown on me, and I didn't want his death on my conscience. I'd dragged him to Cathill's house, he'd saved my life, and in turn I'd put his life in danger.

There were noises all around us now as vans pulled up and more men moved out. More brethren. The cavalry were here, or the clean-up crew depending on which way you looked at it.

There was one hell of a mess to clear up.

CHAPTER 33

TOM TOLD THE ouroboros where she could find her eggs, and thankfully she seemed to understand without Lucy's help. Before she disappeared back underground, she promised no more spontaneous eruptions. There would be no more surprise sink holes in Liverpool; she was going to keep a low profile, as she normally did. She was eager to get back to her eggs and see that they were safe. I couldn't blame her.

The brethren's death toll was far lower than I'd expected, almost exclusively due to Amber who had single-handedly saved nearly a dozen men. Alfie had died, and a man called Giles. Manners would have been the last victim, but he appeared to be healing well. He was still unconscious but his breathing was steady, and his wounds had closed. Emory and I loaded him and the unconscious Lucy into Manners' car, with Gato in tow.

Amber DeLea decided to return to the local coven for a rest and to get supplies to make more containment charms. She would liaise with the elves about the remainder of the daemons. There was nothing left of

Amelia Jane to bury, but Amber wanted to be the one to notify her parents.

We left Tom to direct the clean-up. The heavy cages were being loaded into yet more removal vans, and the malevolent daemons were being taken away. The fewer of us that knew their location the better.

As I drove Manners' car, sleep pulled at me. I opened the windows and let the cold air rush in to keep me awake. To distract me from my exhaustion, Emory told me about his diplomatic ventures. He had spoken successfully to the trolls and the ogres, and both were now aware of the witch's and the piper's duplicity.

Emory had taken Lisette, with him. It had taken no small amount of fast talk on their part, but finally the ogres and the trolls had agreed that Lisette could pipe them into doing nothing other than what they would do naturally. You could only be piped by one piper at a time, so if Lisette was piping them then Sky's corrupt piper couldn't. Their symposium members would be voting *against* the tagging measures; that's what they would have done normally if they hadn't been interfered with.

After all of Emory's careful machinations, the ogres' sense of justice was rough and ready, much like the remainder of the Other realm. Just before 10 p.m., the piper who had sought to control them was found torn limb from limb. A bloody note had been attached to him: *Do not pipe sentient creatures.* The message was clear, albeit a tad brutal for my tastes.

I imagined the piping community would get the message loud and clear. I felt bad for the other pipers; it only took the odd bad egg like Ronan to give them a bad name. It bred distrust and hatred of a species whose skill in talking to animals should be a blessing. Clearly, the Other realmers hadn't seen *Dr Doolittle.*

I pulled up to my house and let out a sigh of relief that I'd managed the drive. I texted Hes to let her know that I was home safe and that the threat to me and my house had been sorted. She could return when she liked, but I warned her that tonight it would be a bit cramped as Lucy and Manners were sleeping over. I didn't get a reply so I assumed she was asleep like any sensible person would be at 1 a.m.

Emory nodded to Chris, who was standing watch outside, and carefully carried Manners into the spare room and laid him on the bed. As I went to move Lucy she stirred and opened bleary eyes. 'Hey,' she said wincing. 'Did we win?'

'We kicked ass and took names,' I promised.

'My head really hurts and I can't feel Esme,' I could hear the panic in her voice.

'You're in the Common,' I reassured her. 'The Other kicked you out. I guess you needed a recharge.'

She blinked. 'Oh.' She looked down at herself, dressed in Emory's suit jacket and nothing else. 'Not a fashion choice I'd roll with,' she said drily.

I shrugged. 'I still think you look hot.'

She laughed a little and nudged me. 'You're the best.' Her smile faded abruptly. 'Lord Samuel...'

'Inside?' I suggested softly.

She nodded. We stood together and walked in, leaning on each other. We must have looked a sight. If the neighbours had seen us, they'd think it had been one hell of a party. They wouldn't be terribly wrong.

Fritz was gently snoring on the sofa in the lounge, surrounded by several laptops that were still running. I covered him with a blanket and took Lucy into the dining room. 'Tea?' I asked.

Lucy nodded, eyes flat. 'Yeah. A cuppa will help, right?'

I gave her another long hug. 'A brew and a cuddle.'

I put the kettle on and my tummy rumbled. Maybe some food would help too. There was some leftover pizza floating about, so I reheated that and did several rounds of toast then took my haul to the dining room.

The house was cold so I flicked on the heating. Emory liked it hot, and I'd got used to my home being warm. I called Chris in; the danger was over, for now, and there was no need for him to stand sentry duty on a cold February night. Plus, he must have been exhausted. It had been a long day for all of us.

We gave him a brief rundown of what had gone

down. His jaw clenched, and his eyes teared up when we told him about Alfie and Giles – he'd known Giles his whole life. I hated being the bearer of bad news. Roll on the cheaters and adulterers, they were so much easier to deal with.

When Emory came downstairs, he knelt down and hugged Gato. 'I'm so sorry,' he murmured. Gato hooked his head around Emory's shoulders, then curled up on the carpet, looking lost. Emory sat next to me, his hand in mine. We were all so tired.

'Food and bed,' I suggested.

For a few minutes we ate in silence before Lucy finally spoke up. 'I have to tell you about Lord Samuel,' she said in a voice so small that I had to strain to hear her.

I set my cup down and gave her my full attention. This wasn't a story she'd want to repeat.

'We were fighting together. Our wolves were so in sync, it was savage and natural and wonderful. A lot of the other wolves were half-hearted, and if they got a good bite or slash, they'd retreat to lick their wounds. But a couple of them were almost crazy. When he was dying, Lord Samuel told me that one of them was Jimmy Rain, the pack leader.

'He fought Jimmy. It was the most savage thing I've ever seen, but they were well matched. Jimmy didn't let up, he was in a haze of bloodlust, and he wanted to tear Lord Samuel to shreds. It was awful. Lord Samuel gave as good as he got, and finally, he gave Rain a deep slash across his belly. Rain limped off to find a healer. Lord Samuel let him go, he was hurt badly too, and then he called me over. We moved away from the other wolves, and Lord Samuel shifted back to human.

'His wounds were so horrific that they weren't healing. He was covered in gashes that smelled wrong. I shifted back, and he told me that Jimmy had dipped his claws in something – a potion or poison – to stop the healing. He said that he was dying.' A tear ghosted down her face and she let it run unchecked.

We remained silent and let her tell the tale. She took a steadying sip of tea and continued. 'He said that if he died by Jimmy's claws, pack law would make Jimmy alpha of our pack. He made me promise that I wouldn't let that happen.' Lucy took a shuddering breath.

My stomach lurched. I was pretty sure I knew now where this story was going.

'The only way to stop Jimmy taking our pack was if someone else killed Lord Samuel. So, at his request, I shifted back to wolf form, and Esme and I slashed his throat. He died quickly by our claws. And we're now alpha of the Home County pack.'

I rose from the table to give her another hug. God knows, she needed it. 'You did the right thing,' I said softly. 'Wilf told me a little about Jimmy Rain, and he was bad news. Wilf wouldn't have wanted his pack to be bound to a wolf like that. He was protecting his pack, protecting you. You did the right thing,' I repeated.

'Then why doesn't it feel right?' Lucy asked plaintively. 'Amber healed so many. She could have healed Lord Samuel if I hadn't already dealt the fatal blow.'

'You can't know that. Amber couldn't heal Manners. If Wilf's wounds were so bad, then I doubt Amber could have done anything for him. You did the right thing, and the right thing is rarely easy. I'm so sorry you had to go through that.'

'I've been a werewolf for a matter of weeks, and now I'm the alpha of a pack. I don't even know what it is to be a wolf. How can I ever hope to lead a pack?'

'Maybe you can abdicate?' I suggested.

Lucy shook her head. 'I know this much about wolf society: there's no stepping down until you're old, until you're an elder. If you want to leave, you're taken down. I'm alpha, or I die.'

I bit my lip. 'Well, it looks like you're alpha then.'

She nodded. 'Yeah. Fuck.'

'You'll be fine. You've always been a fast learner.'

She gave me a wry glance. 'At maths. Not so much at complex social structures.'

I snorted. 'You are the most social person I know. You can read a room in moments, and charm it in seconds. You need to win the wolves over, but if anyone can do that, it's you.'

'Greg will help you,' Emory offered. 'Now he's a wolf, he should be among his own kind. I'll release him from his brethren obligations if he wants me to. You'll be his alpha. He'll have your back – that's just who he is.'

'I'd argue that he should have free will as to where he can go and what he can do,' Lucy said. 'But you're right. He's pack and he needs to be with the pack, the same as I did – as I *do*. And I hope you're right. I could really do with an ally right now.'

'Mrs Dawes and Archie will help you,' I interjected.

She shook her head. 'I'm not so sure of that. I killed Lord Samuel.'

'He was already dying. You just hastened his death to protect the pack. Tell them the truth and they'll help you.'

'Technicality or not, would you help your parents' killers?' Lucy winced. 'Sorry, that was so insensitive of me, I didn't mean—'

I cut her off. 'I know what you meant. Back in the day, when I thought they'd been killed by Bastion, I still helped Bastion save his daughter because it was the right thing to do.'

She sighed. 'You're one of a kind. I doubt Archie will be kindly disposed to me. We'll see.' She squared her shoulders. 'I'm going to bed. I need rest. Tomorrow I'll need to kick ass all over again.'

I kissed her goodnight, and she made her way up to the boxroom to crash out. Chris took the other sofa with the snoring Fritz, and Emory and I went up to my bedroom. We took a hot shower, and I slipped into pyjamas.

I frowned when I went back into my bedroom and couldn't see Gato. 'I'm shattered,' I said to Emory. 'Do you mind if Gato comes up?'

He kissed me gently. 'Not at all. I'll be out in minutes. I'm exhausted.'

I padded back downstairs and found Gato still sitting morosely on the carpet. 'Come on, pup,' I said softly. 'Bedtime.' He seemed to debate for a moment before heaving himself up slowly and following me up the stairs.

I slid into the bed and sidled up next to Emory. He threw an arm around me, already half-asleep. I tapped the bed next to me, and Gato jumped up, turned around three times and lay down beside me.

CHAPTER 34

I AWOKE TO the smell of bacon. I checked the time blearily and was pleasantly surprised to see it was 10 a.m. I had a fast shower to wake myself up then went in hunt of food. Lucy was grilling bacon by the tray load. Emory was drinking coffee in the dining room; he'd showered and shaved and was as immaculate as ever in a black suit and black shirt. His green eyes warmed when he saw me. 'Morning, Jess.'

'I guess it is,' I agreed. 'What's your plan today?'

'Tom is coming to pick me up in ten. I'm going to attend the Connection's vote today.'

'But the dragons aren't part of the Connection.'

'No, but I'm going as part of the troll's delegation.'

I raised an eyebrow. 'To remind everyone of the right way to vote? Are you starting to throw your weight around?'

'Being circumspect hasn't been working too well lately. There's been a conspiracy to poison us, and now a vote to tag us like beasts. Time to start reminding the Connection what will happen if they piss me off.'

'What will happen?' I asked curiously.

Emory smiled unpleasantly. 'The dragons have a huge amount of accumulated wealth. If the Connection wants to fuck with us, we can happily start buying up their infrastructure. We can deny them resources, increase their rental costs, and make life very difficult for them all round. I didn't want to go down that route because it's confrontational and could escalate tensions between the humans and the creatures. But at this point … they can hardly get worse.'

'And if things do get worse?'

'Then all of the creature races that answer to me – and any I can persuade – will pull out of the Connection, making it a toothless organisation of humans. Let them try to dictate to us then.' His tone was grim.

I gave him a kiss. 'Have a great day saving the world.'

'Or destroying it,' he sighed.

'Sometimes you have to knock down to rebuild. Go get them, Emory.' We had another leisurely kiss; I was so pleased that I'd managed to have one more kiss with him.

Fritz and Chris were gone. They'd cleared out early, off to the mysterious brethren headquarters wherever they were. The smell of bacon hadn't just woken me but Manners, too. He was in the kitchen with Lucy, and the tension was high. I stepped in. 'Morning, Toots,' I called to Manners.

His lips twitched. 'That's my line.'

'Yeah, well, it's grown on me.' I gave him a cheeky wink. 'I guess you've had pink hair long enough.' I concentrated, gathering my intention and releasing it. 'Not pink,' I muttered. I really needed to get better with my release commands.

Manner's hair leached from pink back to its usual blond. I studied him; he was broad and muscular, and his grey eyes suited the dirty-blond shade. He hadn't shaved this morning, and a fine layer of stubble graced his square jaw. 'You look better blond,' I admitted.

He winked. 'I can rock any look you throw at me.'

I grinned back. 'Green?'

His grin faltered. 'Maybe let's stick to blond for a bit. My mum didn't love the pink.' That made me giggle. He was so confident that it was hard to imagine him facing his mum's displeasure. 'You don't want to piss my mum off,' he said firmly, 'She's in the Prime's circle of advisors.'

I blinked. 'Is she a dragon?'

He nodded, looking amused. 'I'm brethren, remember? Born to dragons, but a bit of a failure in the dragon gene pool.'

I frowned. 'You're not a failure. The brethren is an essential part of the dragon's social infrastructure. They'd be lost without you all.'

'Wouldn't they just?' he snorted.

'What's your mum's name?'

'Elizabeth.'

'Has Lucy explained…'

'That I'm now a werewolf? Yeah, she mentioned it.' His tone was light but his expression wasn't.

Guilt flared up. I'd taken away his choice, just like I had with Lucy. But still … he wasn't dead. 'How is your mum going to feel about the werewolf thing?' I asked.

'Not warm and fuzzy,' Manner admitted. 'Probably the same as I feel.'

I winced. 'I'm sorry, you were dying, I just—'

'Chill, Jinx. I'd rather be wolfy than dead. It'll take some getting used to, that's all.' He turned to Lucy. 'I am grateful to be alive, to be a wolf.'

Some tension drained out of Lucy. 'Good. That's good. It can be a bit of a shock.'

Manners agreed. 'I'm a soldier so I'm rarely shocked for long. So you're my alpha. What does that mean?'

Lucy squared her shoulders. 'I'm the boss.'

Manners nodded. 'Okay. You're my new prime. What do you need?'

Lucy blinked. 'Huh?'

'How can I help?'

Lucy smiled wryly. 'I have no idea. I'm new to this alpha business. I need an ally.'

'Then you've got it.' Manners snagged a bacon sandwich. 'I'm going to shave, and then we can hit the road. Best leave before my mum gets wind of this.'

'You're making me scared of your mum,' I commented.

'Then you're on a par with the rest of us.' Manner winked, took his sandwich and left Lucy and me alone.

I made myself a sandwich, complete with a generous blob of ketchup. 'This is a good start to the day. I've kissed Emory, my best friend is here and we're having bacon. No one is trying to kill me today.'

Lucy grinned. 'Yeah, that's a good start. I'd better go and pack my bags. I can't have Manners waiting for me.' She looked down at her faded jeans and pale-pink polo shirt. 'Should I change before I go and tell my pack I'm their alpha? Black is the new black, apparently.'

I shook my head. 'You do you. And, Lucy? You might have to do "bitchy back-stabbing you" from high school for a while. No weakness, no fear. Strength and bitchiness. The Other realm is dog eat dog.'

Lucy smirked. 'Don't you worry. Esme and I will crunch away as needed. I didn't get a second chance at life to throw it all away because it's getting tricky. We'll roll with the punches and come up swinging.'

'I know you will. Go get them,' I said for the second time that morning.

Manners and Lucy were packed and on the road shortly after that. It sucked that I already missed her. Maybe I even missed Manners a little. Just a smidge.

I called Hes because I still hadn't had a message back

from her. She answered sounding subdued, and said she was on her way to my house with Nate. They'd be half an hour.

I used that time to give Gato a much-needed shower. He always enjoyed a shower, and afterwards I dried him with a hair dryer, which normally made him roll about in delight. Today, Gato sat patiently, unmoving. I kissed him and scruffled his ears. It would take time to adjust to the new normal, and my heart ached for us all. It was hard to accept that Mum was really gone this time, for good, for real. A part of me expected a second miracle. I hadn't fully accepted my own new reality.

When I came downstairs, Bastion was in my lounge. I bit back a scream of surprise. 'Just let yourself in,' I said drily.

He gave me an amused look but didn't reply. Then his amusement faded and he frowned. He stood up and went over to Gato, touching him lightly. 'Mary?' he said softly.

My eyes filled with tears, and I shook my head. 'To close the portal we needed a sacrifice. Gato and my parents leapt in. We fished Gato out, but not before Mum had departed and started the closure process. Dad's still in there, though.' I said the last part with relief. For most of the last seven years I'd thought my dad was dead too. Now Mum truly was dead, but Dad wasn't. I still had fifty percent of my parental unit left, something to be grateful for no matter the void Mum had left behind.

'I'm sorry, George, Isaac,' Bastion said softly. He gave Gato a gentle stroke, his eyes sad. Then he turned back to me. 'While you were cleaning up, I went to Sky's residence. She kept some detailed logbooks that show she's been blackmailing people. I've sent full details to Emory, but Amelia Jane was one of them. She made a small mistake when she runed someone's house and a home invasion killed the occupants. Sky hushed it up for her, and she's been forcing Amelia Jane to help her ever since.'

'I'll tell Amber. She'll want to know.' Maybe it would help redeem her friend in Amber's eyes. Amber had already lost enough.

Bastion nodded and made as if to leave. 'Woah! Back up, buddy,' I said. 'Did you come all this way just to tell me that? At least stay for a cup of tea.'

The tiniest smile graced his lips. 'You do know that tea doesn't solve all ills?'

'I know you're immortal, but that doesn't mean you're always right.' I stepped closer to my guardian griffin and hugged him. 'Thank you for coming last night.'

'I'm always ready for death and destruction.' He gently removed my arms from his waist. 'Be safe, Jessica Sharp. I'll be seeing you.'

He walked out of the front door just as Hes and Nate

were walking in. Now that Nate was closer, I could feel his anger bubbling away. My eyes widened; I hadn't felt him angry in all the time we'd been bonded. 'Nate? Are you okay?'

He pushed Hes forwards a little and she stumbled. Her eyes were red-rimmed from crying, and she looked miserable. 'What's going on?' I asked.

Hes hung her head a little and Nate glared. She cleared her throat. 'Nate was in the bathroom last night when you texted asking for help. I just – I had a moment of madness. I didn't want Nate to go, didn't want to risk him dying. I'm sorry, I shouldn't have done it. I deleted the message, and I didn't tell him about it.' She started to cry, big fat tears rolling down her cheeks.

'You denied me the right to help my bonded,' Nate snarled furiously.

Hes nodded miserably. She swallowed hard and took a gasping breath. 'I love you,' she tried to explain in a small voice. 'I couldn't bear the thought of you getting hurt! Or worse, dead.'

For a moment, I thought I saw the barest softening in Nate's eyes, and I could feel his anguish streaming down our bond. But as fast as it came, it was overridden by anger. 'I'm already dead, you foolish girl,' he spat out. 'And you've made me foreswear an oath that I gave Jinx. I swore to come to her aid. You have made me an oath-breaker!' He said it like it was the vilest of curses.

I still didn't know enough about vampyr culture to know if oaths were a serious thing, though I recalled Lord Volderiss ripping into his veins and drinking his blood when he took an oath, so yeah … maybe they were something that the vampyrs took pretty seriously.

I didn't know what to say. Perhaps if Nate and some of the Volderiss clan had been there at the battle things would have been different. Maybe Alfie or Giles wouldn't have died. Maybe Stone or my mum might still be alive. Or maybe it would all have shaken out exactly as it had done. Who knew? I said nothing, and Hes sobbed louder.

I turned to Nate. 'I owe you an apology. I thought you didn't come because it was the creatures in the line of fire, and you didn't want to help the brethren – Emory.'

Nate shook his head emphatically. 'No. I would have come.' *True.*

'Well, we're alive – most of us, anyway. It's done now.'

'You're right,' Nate said darkly, looking at Hes. 'It's done now.'

I winced a little as Hes continued to cry. She'd made a foolish mistake, but she didn't know Nate at all if she thought he'd forgive her taking away his choice from him. She was young, naïve and in love – and she'd probably ended her relationship with Nate before it ever really got going.

'Go,' I said to Nate. 'I'll see to her.'

'We're okay?' Nate asked me.

I nodded. 'Of course. Even if you'd *chosen* not to come, we would still have been okay. It's always your choice.'

'I would have come,' he reiterated, glaring at Hes. 'Please pass my apologies to Emory.'

'Of course I will.'

With one last look at Hes, Nate walked out, slamming the front door. I wondered if he admitted to himself the regret that he felt at that moment. He might be angry with Hes, but that didn't mean he'd stopped loving her.

I put an arm around Hes. 'Not your wisest decision,' I said softly. 'Come on. Let's sort you out.'

CHAPTER 35

IN THE END I sent Hes back to university. Something between us had permanently shifted. I had believed – had sworn to Amber – that I could trust Hes, but now I couldn't. That changed things. I wasn't sure if we could still work together, but firing her for one lapse of judgement seemed like overkill. She was young and in love, and she'd made a decision, however wrongly, to protect Nate. I'd give her another chance but the total trust was gone.

I logged into work and answered a few emails. I checked my insurance claim for my Mercedes. I took Gato for a walk. After all the turmoil of the last few days, normality was nice. I went to the shops and bought some food. I wasn't much of a cook – I could burn water – but I could make Bolognese pasta.

I made it to my mum's recipe, and the smell filled the house and made me cry. I sobbed on the kitchen floor while Gato whined next to me. I burned the Bolognese. I was just throwing it in the bin when Emory came home. He saw my tear-streaked face and quickly pulled me into a silent hug.

Words of comfort are a strange thing. Sometimes they make me furious; '*Be grateful for what time you had*' or '*Think of all the happy memories*' make me want to punch someone. They are no consolation and, for me, silence is better. Emory was familiar with loss, and he recognised that. I needed his support and I had it.

'I burnt dinner,' I confessed.

'Japanese food?' Emory suggested.

I smiled. 'Sounds good.'

Emory told me about the vote. It had gone our way, of course; there would be no tagging for the creatures. After Bastion had delivered Sky's logbooks to Emory, discreet notes had been sent to the blackmail victims to let them know that she was dead, as was her hold over them. They were asked to vote with their conscience and they did. The vote wasn't even close, a fact that pleased the creatures greatly, though it was still a sore point that the bill had even been introduced. It helped appease the creatures that both its sponsors, Stone and Sky, were dead.

I told Emory that Stone had changed his mind, that he was going to support us. Emory's face was dubious, but he didn't argue with me.

Stone's death hadn't really sunk in. He'd been an integral part of my introduction to the Other, and compulsion aside, we'd shared laughter and an electric kiss. I'd honestly hoped that we would reconnect as friends one day, maybe after he'd married Elvira. She was going to be heartbroken. Although the vote had been a success, I couldn't help but think of Alfie's and Giles' families, and even Sky's. Perhaps she hadn't been a stone-cold bitch to them.

'What do we do now the bill has failed?' I asked Emory.

'I don't know. Celebrate?' he suggested.

'Yeah, that too. But what do we do? How do we bridge this divide between the creatures and the humans?'

He shook his head. 'It isn't a small divide that we can bridge. It isn't a crack in the pavement, it's a gaping abyss. It's a centuries-old problem, Jinx. I don't know the answer.'

'Old age hasn't brought you wisdom yet, huh?' I teased.

'I'm still very young by dragon standards. It's a miracle they made me Prime.'

'They recognised that times are changing, and they need someone to help them change with them,' I suggested.

'Maybe. Or maybe they just wanted a scapegoat.'

'If that's what they wanted, they've failed miserably. You're doing a great job.'

'Thanks.' He kissed me. 'You always make me feel better.'

'That's because we're a kick-ass team. There's nothing we can't do if we put our minds to it.' I linked my hands with his.

'And you want us to put our minds to bridging the gap?'

'Yes. Don't you ever go on the Underground in London where they keep saying "please mind the gap"? The warning is there. We need to mind the gap, Emory, or who knows what the future will bring to our people.'

He flashed me a two-hundred-watt smile.

'What?' I asked.

'You said "our" people.'

I rolled my eyes. 'Of course I said our people. We're bonded, you and I. What's mine is yours, etc.'

'You're right,' Emory agreed. 'So how about we take one of your ideas for a spin?'

'One of my ideas?'

'With a twist, of course.'

'Which idea?' I asked curiously.

Emory squeezed my hand and then released it. He looked at Gato, who nodded, then reached into his pocket and pulled out a small white box. He went down on one knee and opened it. Inside was a classically beautiful ring with a diamond big enough to have its own gravitational field. 'How about instead of Mr and Mrs Shite, we try Mr and Mrs Elite? Jessica Sharp, will you marry me?'

I burst into tears and threw myself into his arms.

'Is that a yes?' he murmured against my lips.

I nodded, still sobbing. Eventually I managed to croak a 'Yes!'.

Emory drew back. 'With Lucy's help, I asked your parents' permission to ask you.'

A knot took residence in my throat. 'That's adorable, in an old-fashioned way.'

'I am adorable,' he confirmed, ignoring the 'old-fashioned' part. 'Your mum gave her blessing, Jess, and your dad, too. If you want, your dad could walk you down the aisle.'

Gato leapt up, barking and wagging his tail enthusiastically.

I smiled at my dog-father sadly. My mum would have loved to have seen me married, but she'd seen me happy, and she'd met Emory. It was enough; it had to be.

Gato let out a soft whine. I guess it didn't take a genius to see where my thoughts had gone. I managed a tremulous smile. I had my father, and that was a blessing I'd thought I'd never have again. I could almost hear my mum in my ear murmuring, 'Onwards and upwards, darling.'

I managed a stronger smile. 'Yes,' I repeated to Emory. 'Mrs Elite has grown on me.'

He slid the ring onto my finger. I wasn't an ostentatious person but, despite its size, the rock looked right.

Something in me settled.

Emory linked his hands with mine. 'Well then, I guess I'd better introduce you to my court.' He laughed loudly. 'Those poor bastards. They're not going to know what's hit them.'

GLIMMER OF WHAT IS NEXT

Don't panic! This series is complete because we FINAL-LY know what happened to Jinx's parents. But Jinx and Emory's tale is far from complete…

And watch out for a certain alpha werewolf, who needs to navigate tricky waters – luckily, she'll have a certain ill *mannered* individual to help guide her…

Subscribe to my newsletter, follow my Facebook Author Page or join my Facebook Group (Heather G Harris' Other Realm) for the very latest news!

ACKNOWLEDGEMENTS

In finishing up this series, the biggest thanks have to go to my amazing editor. She's helped me so much, not just in the actual editing, but in endless support. Every time I've battled Imposter Syndrome, there she is, telling me I'm actually a Good Writer. Thanks Karen, my very own Jinx.

ABOUT THE AUTHOR

Heather is an urban fantasy writer and mum. She was born and raised near Windsor, which gave her the misguided impression that she was close to royalty in some way. She is not, though she once she got a letter from the Queen's lady-in-waiting.

Heather went to university in Liverpool, where she took up skydiving and met her future husband. When she's not running around after her children, she's plotting her next book and daydreaming about vampyrs, dragons and kick-ass heroines.

Heather is a book lover who grew up reading Brian Jacques and Anne McCaffrey. She loves to travel and once spent a month in Thailand. She vows to return.

Want to learn more about Heather? Subscribe to her newsletter for behind-the-scenes scoops, free bonus material and a cheeky peek into her world. Her subscribers will always get the heads-up about the best deals on her books.

Newsletter: heathergharris.com/subscribe
Follow her Facebook Page: facebook.com/Heather-G-Harris-Author-100432708741372
Instagram: instagram.com/heathergharrisauthor
TikTok: tiktok.com/@heathergharris
Contact info: www.HeatherGHarris.com
HeatherGHarrisAuthor@gmail.com

REVIEWS

Reviews feed Heather's soul. She'd really appreciate it if you could take a few moments to review her book and say hello.